Zephyr

By

Huckleberry Rahr

ISBN eBook: 978-1-959981-69-5
ISBN paperback: 978-1-959981-70-1

Editor: Weslee Imrisek
Developmental Editor: Angela Grimes
Cover Art: Getcovers.com
Formatting: Huckleberry Rahr

Books in the Pebble Stone Series

1: Xenagogue

2: Yugen

3: Zephyr

Books by Huckleberry Rahr

- Jade Stone Chronicles
  - Wolf Healer
  - Epsilon
  - Alphas
  - Traitor
  - Pack
  - Battlefield
  - Pack Present
- Pebble Stone Chronicles
  - Xenagogue
  - Yugen
  - Zephyr
- Ember Savita Chronicles
  - Veiled Phoenix
  - Moonstone Phoenix
  - Battle Phoenix
- Hidden Magic Series (working titles ...)
  - The Aura of The Chameleon
  - The Chameleon's Duplicity
  - Truth Exposed
- The Search – Short Story, eBook only

Acknowledgements

To all the readers who've stuck with me from the beginning of the Jade Stone Chronicles, thank you! To all the readers who are new, thank you! I am so appreciative of each and every one of you. I started writing for my son, but I continued writing for the readers.

A special shout out goes out to the usual suspects, Wes, Angela, and Elizabeth. You three will read all my ramblings, regardless of how incoherent, and help me bring joy and heart to my words ... and more variation of words.

I'd also like to give a special thank you to Dulaine. You've stuck with me since the start with this series. By now, you've become an inner circle helper, and I really appreciate your help.

Unless something big happens, this will be the end of Jade and Pebble's stories. I have new tales to tell.

Huckle

To The Readers

Zephyr is the last book in the Pebble Stone Chronicles. This trilogy can be read as a separate series from the Jade Stone Chronicles. That said, there are spoilers in this series since it takes place after the end of Jade's books.

Chapter 1 – A Decision

"Because, Pebble." Jade's voice, as she sat across from me in the pack office, was low and full of concern. That worried me more than just about anything else. "Quinn recognized Trista. She used to be one of the kids of the Dynasty."

The Dynasty? The group that tried to eliminate the California pack. Rogue wolves that called themselves a family but were really just egocentric bullies? The wolves that Jade, Bevin, and José spent their first years as leaders of the California pack having to deal with? The same Dynasty that shouldn't be around anymore? Trista was one of them?

A cold chill froze my body. My mind played over every interaction I'd had with her. Each one of her words and actions.

What do I really know about her?

Clarity hit me, and I slowly blinked. Thoughts whirled in my head, and I patted myself down as I searched for my phone. It wasn't in my pockets. *When did I last have it?*

"Jade," I snapped my eyes to hers, finally focusing back on the here and now, "can I use your phone?"

"Of course. Who do you need to call?" She held out the small device. "Tanner? Quinn? Bevin? I have all the numbers saved under contacts."

My hand stopped halfway to hers and what she held out to me. Then a snarl escaped my lips. "I don't know her number."

"Whose number, and where's your phone?" Despite the tornado of emotions crashing through me, Jade sounded calm and collected.

Gods, I'm glad she's here.

Taking my hand back, I massaged my temples. "I need to talk with Luna. We have a real battle on our hands. I can't have someone in the pack—in the house— who's not with us. Especially when she's been working so hard to actively antagonize me. I just can't with her and that ... not right now. No more games. I need to know where she stands. I told her she'd have until after the first full moon run, but this changes everything. It's not fair, but, then again, when has the Dynasty ever made things easy for anyone?" My jaw and fists clenched. I closed my eyes and forced myself to breathe, relax.

Again, I wondered why my wolf thought Luna was the perfect match for me. Since meeting the feisty red-head at the start of the semester, she and I had clashed. The only times I'd seen her act anything but arrogant was when interacting with Dayna or other people she considered hers. From what I could tell, that behavior belonged to the goose shifters.

After her mom saw the connection between us and she begrudgingly returned to Wisconsin, the two of us shared aspects of powers other alphas possessed. Despite that, Luna continued to fight our joining to lead the pack.

Part of me saw how she treated Dayna, and even Conner, and yearned for that. Another part wanted the stress of her constant presence gone. If she'd leave, I could hone my focus where it needed to be.

Jade reached out and placed a hand on my wrist. The touch of family slowed my heart, and I took a breath as the tremble in my arms receded.

I smiled up at her and continued. "Once I have her sorted, I need to talk with Tanner." I pulled out a piece of paper and pencil, and started to doodle, hoping the random marks would help my mind to focus. "Then, I'll want to talk with Quinn." I gazed back up at her. "You're welcome to attend that second meeting. Finally, I have the alpha meeting at eight." I worried my head would explode with everything on my list and no time to do it all.

"Listen to you, sis. You sound so in control of everything. I'm proud." Her smile warmed me to my toes and something deep within me relaxed. *Gods, it's good to have her here.*

Despite her sentiment, I felt anything but like I knew what was going on. Saying the words out loud helped me to pull the ideas from the cyclone going on within me. To Jade, I just smiled, trying to keep the outside calm. "Now, I just need to implement all this."

She stood and came around the desk, engulfing me in a hug. "Why don't I go find Luna? I'll send her up. Then, I'll find your phone. Where did you last have it? And since when do you misplace things, especially your phone?"

"First off, yes, please. I'll take all the help I can get. I really need to speak to Luna. Next, I know I had it when I ate, but then you came to tell me about the babies." Instinctively I patted my pockets again. "I can't believe I didn't immediately slip it back in a pocket. I can't fathom not having my phone on me now. I fought Mom and Dad too hard to get a phone to randomly leave it somewhere. If it's not in the kitchen, ask Tyler. He's been the lead on the security for all our devices for a few years now. He should be able to locate it."

Jade left the room, and I began to pace. My hands trembled so I shook them, trying to get my body under control. I had to figure things out, make a lot of big decisions, and do all of this without my nerves showing, especially in front of Luna. Just what I needed, one more thing for her to critique.

You have one more minute, Pebble, then get yourself under control. You are the alpha.

I laughed at my own ridiculousness. But at the same time, I knew I wasn't wrong. *And now you're talking to yourself about yourself. Get yourself together!*

With a big exhalation, I stopped moving. The stillness of the office seeped into me as I slowly turned and leaned onto the desk, breathing deeply to slow my heart. My eyes closed and I took stock of my situation.

Wolf, are there any other people in the pack I need to worry about?

Unlike Jade, I couldn't carry on an actual conversation with my wolf, but I could get impressions and premonitions. We had a different relationship than most werewolves had with their animal side. The pressure that built behind my breastbone was warm and soothing. A cessation of worry.

Part of me debated trusting my wolf. After she chose Luna, I wondered if complete belief in all things she said was the right move, but for now I decided to stay the course.

I didn't know how long I sat there letting my body settle, but my private moments with my wolf were interrupted by a knock at the door. The sound shocked me, and I jerked to my feet.

Luna stood alone, statuesque and gorgeous. If only she were as pleasant to interact with as she was to look at. She gave off a cinnamon apple scent, annoyed and curious. I beckoned, and she entered. "Your sister sent me up. Is there a meeting now I don't know about? Are we waiting for others?" She sounded exasperated, like she just wanted this to be over.

As her questions washed over me, I went back to perching on the desk. I decided sitting behind the desk was too formal. I wanted Luna to feel at ease. "We need to talk. It needs to be private. And it needs to be now."

Her step only faltered for a second before she got to a chair and sat. Then one eyebrow rose. My jaw clenched at the implied annoyance, but I didn't care. We had to come to a resolution. Luna's voice came out tight. "What is this about?"

I slumped, sighing. For so many reasons, I didn't want to have this conversations. But at this point, I didn't see any other option. "It feels like it's been months, but in reality we've known about each other's animals for only a few weeks."

Her only reaction was a small shoulder raise. She had the best poker face I'd ever seen ... no other emotion showed on her expression. Despite that, I gave her a few seconds, just to make sure she didn't want to add anything, then I continued. "I told you, gods, last weekend? That feels like a lifetime ago as well, that you would have time to make a decision about this pack and your position in it."

"You said I'd have until after the first full moon run, which is in two days." Her tone wasn't quite as snappish as usual, but there was a bit of an edge.

"Right. That's what I said." I couldn't respond to her tone with anything similar. That would be childish and start a disagreement. Not only did we not have time for that, I knew I had to be alpha. It was time.

Trying to stay calm, I rubbed my face. "Things have changed, Luna. I can't wait." She tensed as if to interrupt, but I held up a hand to stop her. "Look, I know one of the wolves who is attacking the pack. I need to create a plan." Her eyes widened as I spoke. "The pack can't know who the attacker is for now ... except for a few people. I need to know if you're planning on stepping up, accepting the mantle, and becoming a leader. If you are, I'll invite you to the rest of the discussions. If not," I shook my head. "This is too big and important to play around. Lives have been lost and more could be added to that count. This isn't a game. It's life or death."

Luna's mouth opened and closed a few times as her eyes bored into me. "You know who one of the jerks killing off innocents is, and we're in here discussing politics?" Her eyes narrowed as she gazed up towards the corner of the ceiling and mumbled. "It's Trista ... isn't it." Then she shook her head. "No, I retract that. I get it. So, just to be clear, what exactly do you need from me?"

Teeth clenched, I blew out some air, then said, "I need you to decide, Luna. Are you going to join the pack and take up the alpha mantle? Do you want to work with me to lead the Wisconsin werewolf pack? Do you want to become my partner in making big decisions that could affect the lives of many people?" There was so much more I wanted to ask, to put on the table, to say. But in the end, that was the heart of what I needed to know.

My throat tightened and my eyes burned with unshed tears as I thought about what I would lose if she didn't say 'yes'. I'd never have what my parents had, or Bevin and José. I'd never have the love my siblings had found, but in the end, if I could keep the pack safe, that was what was important. My whole life was about my wolf—why should this be any different?

She leaned back in her seat, her head tilting to the side as she gazed at me. "Part of me really wants to wait until after the full moon run and see what that feels like, but I understand that at this point, that's not possible. I also know from sitting in that ridiculous room twice for those wacky meetings—in two weeks no less—that this large mass of people feels like family. It was there before I had a wolf, but today ... it felt like a family meal—funny, annoying, obnoxious, but—" her mouth pursed closed for a moment, "—kind of wonderful in the end. It surprised me both times." The last came out a bit softer, as if she were in a daze.

A smile played across my face. I knew what she meant. As much as the pack meetings were a chore, part of me loved them. Everyone got together, talked, debated, and freely gave their opinions. Our pack was safe, and those meetings proved how strong a family we were. It was all the proof I'd ever need that Wisconsin had the strongest and most stable werewolf pack in the country.

Luna continued. "After the meeting, Dayna and I spoke about joining. You know Dayna's opinion. She's wanted to be a wolf her whole life. I told her I was in. She asked when I would tell you. Since Jade and Brooke are here and you've been distracted, I thought I'd just wait until after the run, like we originally discussed." She bit her lower lip. It was the sincerest and realest I'd ever seen her. "But, yes, Pebble, I do want in. I want to be part of this large, wacky pack ... this family." Before I could respond, she held up her hand, much as I had before. "And in here," she tapped her chest, "I feel the need to protect them all."

I knew that feeling; it was part of the alpha power, wanting to be free to connect with the wolves of the pack. The corners of my mouth twitched as I bit back a cheer. "Okay, we should go down to the living room and do this with as many people as are still here. The pack would be disappointed if they missed it."

"What is 'this'?"

"You're getting your alpha mantle, of course."

Chapter 2 – Snake In The Grass

Luna and I headed down the stairs to the main level. There were people all over the house, but most were still in the living room.

When I got halfway down, I whistled and everyone gaped at me. Jade poked her head from the kitchen and waved, then continued doing what she'd been doing—either searching for my phone or people. "I have an announcement—"

On one loveseat, Chris scoffed. "Another one? Didn't we already have a full meeting?"

Uncle Jackson winked up at me. "Or does this mean we'll get more food, like, with each additional announcement, we get an extra dessert?"

Everyone laughed.

Happiness bubbled up, warming what had been chilled within me from the earlier news. "Yes, another one. Can someone gather everyone scattered about the den? I don't want to go to the meeting room if we don't have to. And as for sugars, if you really want that, I'll get Jade to go bake while we talk."

Everyone groaned. Brooke shook her head. "Have mercy on us all." My sister was notorious for not being the best cook. She wasn't actually bad, but the running gag made everyone happy, much like the one about her and geese. The pack liked all the inside jokes about each other—we really were a big dorky family.

Andy dramatically put his arm around Chris. "So, you're saying we don't have to move?"

"Yes, that's what I'm saying."

His eyes twinkled. "Well, then, fearless leader, I am not opposed to this announcement, no matter what my husband says." He swung his head towards my aunt and uncle sitting across from them. "And I don't need to be bribed with Jade's ... whatever it is she does in the kitchen—disaster or otherwise."

"Hey!" Jade's voice came from the other room, full of indignation.

While we bantered, the rest of the pack slowly filled the room.

Chris narrowed his eyes at Andy. "I just didn't want to move from this very comfortable couch."

Uncle Jackson harrumphed. "Are you saying the meeting room couches aren't comfortable? Is our pack house not good enough for you anymore?"

After a beat, Chris threw his head back and laughed. "I would never critique the pack den of the best pack in the nation." His gaze took in all the people milling around the room. "Or the fancy couches." He leaned forward. "Though, I will say, some of them do seem better suited for gazing upon then sitting on. This one." His hand slapped down hard. "This is a sitting couch."

"Okay!" I said loudly enough to cut across them, and the others who started to join in. "I know you want to get back to the food but let me say this."

Everyone gazed up at me.

"When my wolf started giving me premonitions about Luna, it was that she'd be the one to help me lead this mutt-ly crew." There were chuckles. "Despite that, I wanted the decision to be hers, not the vision my wolf had. Today, she's made up her mind ... despite the clowns on the couch." All around, the wolves' eyes practically glowed with their excitement.

Andy groaned loudly. "Please tell me it had nothing to do with the earlier meeting. Chris will become unbearable if he thinks he had anything to do with the decision."

"Oh," I said with grave sincerity, "it had nothing to do with Chris."

The emotions in the room were light and festive, and the scent of vanilla filled the area. Despite the looming threat of Trista and the Dynasty, my mood echoed theirs. Searching the faces, I wanted to make sure everyone, or at least the majority, of the pack was present. As I slowly cataloged who was there, I saw Jade near the entrance to the kitchen with Tanner and Clare. She smiled and gave a thumbs up. Brooke still sat on the couch with the computer open. *I wonder if the California pack is listening.*

Halfway through my perusal, I saw Trista standing in the back near the door. Thinking about her, I realized her connection to me was muted, I could barely pinpoint her. *Is this something she's doing? She seems to have an understanding of the pack bonds most wolves don't possess.*

She smiled and waved. It took a beat, but I forced myself to smile back. Then I finished my count. "I don't know how many of you know what it takes to go from potential alpha to true alpha. Most of it happened when Luna made the decision a few minutes ago. The rest is her deciding in front of all of you."

Uncertain how she'd react, I reached back and slid my hand into hers. It trembled, but she allowed me to help steady her. "As chaotic as the pack meeting was," Luna said, a wide smile on her face, "it felt like home. I knew then that I wanted to be alpha with Pebble. I hope I can be the kind of alpha all of you are proud of. Thank you for giving me this opportunity."

As her voice trailed off, everyone applauded.

Within me, something relaxed as I realized how sincere Luna sounded. She'd spoken from her heart in a way everyone could hear. There was no arrogance or snide tone in what she'd said. It was like a whole new person stood with me. I could almost cry as hope threatened to overwhelm my senses.

When it was done, I signaled Jade, Tanner, and Clare, then turned to head back to the office, Luna in tow.

This time when I got into the office, I sat in the big chair. "Luna, can you pull a chair around and sit near me?" There would be more people, and we needed to have a serious talk. Within a few minutes, everyone sat staring at me.

After pulling off the page of doodles from the pad of paper, I turned to Jade. "Is the door closed? And did you find my phone?"

"Yes and no."

"Okay, in that case we'll need Tyler at this meeting as well."

Leaning back in his seat, Tanner's expression hardened—he had his game face on. He pulled out *his* phone and tapped a few quick strokes. "He's on his way."

Once the last member of what I thought of as my inner circle sat in the room, I gazed into their eyes. "Some of you know Quinn Verater from the California pack. He and his twin started off as Dynasty kids before they met

Jade at college. The Dynasty had a lot of young, almost as many as they had odd ideas about werewolves and pack."

Luna shook her head. "What is this 'Dynasty?'"

"A long story." I sighed. "I'll fill you in on the entire history after this meeting. Suffice it to say, when the California pack started up, they bumped into a cult of werewolves, and it wasn't pretty." I licked my lips. I hated having to admit how wrong I'd been about Trista over the last few months. She'd been in my head, and I hadn't realized who she was. "When I was speaking to Owen over the computer, Quinn collected one of the babies. He looked at the screen to say 'hi' to me. Trista walked past behind me. He recognized her. She comes from California, not Tennessee, and not Florida—like she told us at different times. She's originally from San Mateo. She's one of them. A Dynasty wolf."

The ginger scent of shock permeated the office. Though Luna smelled of jasmine, smug satisfaction. She had predicted Trista, after all.

Finally, Clare's face tightened. "What is she doing here? And wasn't one of the pillars of that awful sexist pack that women couldn't become wolves? How is she a wolf?"

"I've been thinking about that." All the eyes in the room, filled with heat and frustration, turned to me. "We need to get more details from Quinn, but if her family complained at all about the California pack before she left, then she would know. From the beginning, Jade had always been a main target. Because of that, she would know females could become wolves."

Across from me Jade nodded. "It's true. Part of the reason that cult hated us was they thought we'd corrupted one of their females."

As we spoke, Luna's face scrunched up in disgust. I could only agree with the look. I continued. "Trista would also know that her family had been destroyed by a group of wolves that had originated here in Wisconsin. She's only a bit older than me, so all of this would've happened when she was twelve, thirteen, maybe fourteen. These are pivotal years in a kid's development. She's probably been harboring a hatred for our pack as well as the California family, for years."

A big sigh gushed from Tanner. "That sounds logical. I can't imagine having so much hate for strangers. But you also may be thinking too small. She may hate *all* pack wolves. She and her group are starting here, but she may hope to bring all the organized wolves down."

Luna tilted her head. "Did they start here? Wasn't Tennessee hit first?"

My head fell back as I tried to piece together the timeline. When I had my thoughts organized, I rubbed my eyes and searched the faces of those in the room.

Tyler grunted, distracting me from whatever it was I was seeing on their faces. "Knowing all of this is interesting, but why am I here? I've never been part of one of these meetings."

Everyone looked back at him, then to me. *I'm alpha, I can't be distracted by trivialities.* "I can't find my phone. The last time I remember having it was eating in the kitchen. As it goes, I happen to have been sitting next to Trista. I also don't know how they've been finding us so easily. They must be utilizing technology. We need to be ahead of them. That's you."

Rubbing her forehead, Luna mumbled softly, "Why didn't you tell anyone before this meeting? She was there at the announcement. What if she's gone?"

"Got it." Though Tyler spoke to me, he was staring down at his phone. "Your phone is off. I can't find it on the map. I'll put someone on a twenty-four-hour watch. I'll get you a burner phone. Unless you want a new phone; I can arrange that as well."

"A burner is fine for now." I wrote things down, keeping myself organized.

He nodded. "I'll work with Tanner and one of my specialists. Once we know where Trista is, we'll get her tagged and bugged—car, phone, and any place she's bedding down. It'll take a few days."

"I agree with Luna, why didn't you have Jade tell us you'd been eating with her? We could've asked her about the phone. My guess is she's long gone." Tanner's voice was somewhere between respectful and a snarl.

Fighting the sense of dread, the feeling of messing up before I'd even started, I took a moment to allow my emotions to play out. A gentle hand on my leg centered me. I gazed down to see Luna had used the power of pack to calm me and suddenly I could breathe. In my head I heard, *Family ... just answer. You're fine.*

The shock of Luna giving me a pep talk took another second to acclimate. Then I nodded at Tanner and said, "You're right. I was processing a lot, and I know that's not an excuse. Moving forward I will have all of you to help me with the things that are going on. I'll try not to make a mistake like that again."

Tanner's mouth twitched slightly, the kind of tell most people missed. "Very good."

Clare looked contemplative. "We want Fern to go to their Dad to speak to him. We also want to have someone go with them, right?"

And that was a whole other issue. My new friend from college who happened to be the child of lone wolves who used to be part of the Tennessee pack. If we could convince them to return to Tennessee, then Mom and Dad could come home and I, we—me and Luna—could go back to just being students. As much as I loved the idea of being alpha of the best pack ever, waiting until after graduation sounded better.

While everyone spoke, I continued to take notes. In future meetings, I'd probably assign someone else to the task, but writing helped me to process information, so, for now, I needed to do this myself. I wanted to make sure I knew everything that was discussed and decided. "Yes. Tanner said he'd choose who would accompany Fern. I know they wanted me to go, but I need to be here to lead."

"Right," Clare said, nodding. "But Luna just took up the mantle. She can babysit the pack, which mostly runs on its own. She'll have all of us here—well, not Jade, she's leaving tomorrow—but the rest of us. My guess is you are high on Trista's hit list. You and Fern. If the two of you are out of town, then that's two fewer wolves to protect."

I bristled, gazing at her. "You do know I can protect myself. I took down the two who attacked Fern and Hollis when we went out the other night. Dad's training has paid off."

For a moment, I thought about Hollis, my best friend since starting public school, and her awful introduction to the world of werewolves. *Will she ever forgive me? Have I lost her forever?*

"When you know there's an attack coming, yes. But if they do what they did to the Tennessee alphas, we'd lose another alpha," she persisted. "Since I know Fern prefers you going with them, are you against it?"

I looked at Luna who watched and listened but didn't seem intimidated. "What do you think? You just agreed to leadership. What's your opinion about my leaving for a few days after the moon run?"

After searching my expression for a moment, she gazed around the room, taking in each person. Then she faced me again. "If that will help in this situation, then go. I'll do what the pack needs me to do. Dayna and Conner will be here as well, and you know they'll be happy to help me."

That made me smile. It was true. She had her own posse. "Okay, we have a plan. Now, Jade," I swung around to face her. "Can you call Quinn? I'd like to know who Trista is." The look of pride Jade gave me as she pulled out her phone and made the call filled me with the love of family, something I'd been missing since all of this had started, and it helped to ground me.

The phone only rang a couple times before Quinn picked up. "Jade?"

Jade nodded at me, letting me know I had lead. "Hi, Quinn. It's me, Pebble. I'm here with a group of people. I was hoping we could ask you a few questions."

"Hiya, Pebble. What can I help you with?"

"Can you tell me about Trista?" A tension built in the room, and everyone leaned towards the phone.

"Trista? I'm not sure I know who you're talking about."

Biting back a growl, I gazed at the ceiling for a moment. "The wolf you saw. Um, Elizabeth?" *That was the name, right, wolf?* My chest warmed with approval.

"Oh, right, Elizabeth! Beth. She was younger than me. This is one of those times I wish my sister was here." A wave of bitter earthy scent wafted from Jade. She still felt guilty and sad over that situation all these years later. I shot her a look, but she just shook her head. "She always watched the neighbor kids. There were a bunch of them, and I didn't know them all." I could hear Quinn's hesitancy. "I'm trying to remember her exact details. If not that, then, wait, let me start from the top. The Dynasty had a safe house in Utah. We were told to go there if there was ever anything dangerous happening. My guess is mothers with kids were sent there."

A weight filled me. "Do you have any idea how many that may have been?"

"I don't." A pained sound came over the line. "I realize that doesn't help, but I honestly don't think that all the kids would follow Beth in her vendetta. A lot of what the Dynasty was and believed in was kept from the youth. Some knew if their parents spoke about it, but mostly we were just kids until we graduated high school. And if a family only had girls, they may never know what was going on."

Luna's head tilted. "Does Trista, er Beth, have a brother? How would she know about the werewolves?"

Again, Quinn grunted. "I can't tell you. As a male of the Dynasty, I wasn't asked to watch the kids. That was always put on my sister. The Dynasty was extremely sexist, but you know that."

A cinnamon scent of annoyance filled the room. Not at Quinn, but at the idea of this group. Luna's face scrunched up. "This Dynasty that you're all talking about, it's gone, right? No more," she waved a hand, "of all of this stupidity?"

Jade huffed out a laugh. "Oh, yeah. We took down the heads of that hydra ... years ago. They are no longer a cult, trust me."

"Good." The conviction in Luna's voice had me smiling in approval. It was nice having her ire directed at someone else.

"Thank you, Quinn. I may call if I have more questions, but I think that's what we needed."

"Any time, Pebble. I'm glad I could help."

Once Jade hung up, I leaned back and smiled. "Okay, we have a game plan for the next few days. Unless Trista realized Quinn recognized her, which I doubt since she was still here when Luna was announced as alpha, we should be able to start tracking her Tuesday when she comes for the moon run. Wednesday, I'll head to Kentucky with Fern while all of you find the rest of her group. When I get back, we end this."

Chapter 3 – New Sheriff in Town

Tyler was the first to stand. "I assume you don't want anyone to know about anything we discussed in this meeting."

A smile flashed on my face. "Correct. These meetings should be kept confidential. I'm sorry, I should've mentioned that when you came in."

"Not a problem. I figured that when I was invited in." His hand landed on the door handle, and he looked around. "I've never been in here before. It's impressive."

He winked. "Anyway, I'll get you a phone later tonight or by tomorrow at the latest."

"Thanks again, Tyler."

He grunted, then left the room.

With a tight face, Luna leaned forward. "I have a question. I don't know if I should just wait and ask Pebble when we're alone or ask all of you." The muscles across her back were all tense.

Apprehension filled me. "What's the topic?"

"The mantle."

I relaxed into my seat like a blanket being pulled off me. "Go ahead, ask."

She shook her head. "I don't understand what it is. You said I have it now, but what are you talking about?"

"Right, you've only been in the pack a week. Close your eyes and think about your wolf."

All four people around me followed my directions. I felt like a teacher in front of an exclusive class. "Now, your wolf naturally keeps guards up so that the other wolves can function. It's our power source. Think of a guard or a blanket or maybe curtains that you can pull back. As you remove it, your power will be apparent to everyone around you."

Like a light switch being thrown, Luna's power flooded the room. Both Tanner and Clare grasped the arms of the chairs they sat in, sweat dotting their forehead. Jade's breathing slowed, as the power thickened the air. I felt the power and let it wash through me, impressed with her level.

"Okay, Luna." My voice was loud, as if speaking over a group. It was silent, but the intensity she yielded was a force that made me feel like I needed to speak up. "Put the cover back over your wolf."

Her eyes snapped open, and she took in the others in the room. She gasped, and the strength she held no longer filled the room. "But I've felt you use a bit of your power before." Luna's eyes were wild as she gaped at me. "What did I do wrong?"

The others in the room visibly relaxed as Luna and I discussed what happened.

"Nothing." I couldn't help chuckling. It was nice to have something so mundane to focus on for a minute. "This was your first time dealing with your mantle and werewolf oomph. It's something I've grown up with. You'll learn and I'll help." I turned to Tanner. "I'll get the other alphas caught up at the meeting at eight. I'm trusting you, Easton, and Tyler with finding out everything you can about Trista ... or Beth, or whoever she is."

A small smile played across Tanner's face. "Sounds like a plan, boss." He turned to Clare. "I assume you can follow her finances."

"I'll put Estrella on that. It's good practice for her."

The emotions of all the pack still played in the back of my mind. I closed my eyes and tried to home in on Trista, but she was buried under everyone else. As before, when I focused on her, it felt like she was trying to veil, or as if she were moving away.

"Okay, I think we're done here." I pushed myself up. "Luna, we should meet back up here a bit before eight so we can be ready for the meeting. Everyone else, thank you for being here. I think we have a plan. If anything comes up in tonight's meeting, I'll let you know Tuesday before the run. If it's more urgent, I'll get a hold of you tomorrow."

On her way out, Luna turned and gave me a smile. I nearly fell over in shock, and she smirked at whatever expression I made. Spinning on her heel, she sauntered off. *Well, at least I know not everything's different.*

Once everyone but Jade left, she came over and gave me a hug. "I've never sat through one of these meetings with Mom and Dad, but I've been in a few in California. You did great, sis."

"Thanks. I kind of feel like I've been thrown into the deep end of a pool, or maybe dropped into the ocean, and forgot how to swim." Despite my words, a feeling of calm resolution settled on me. A lot was happening, but I felt like we had a plan. And as much as I hated to admit it, having Luna in my corner helped. Not only was I not alone, she'd bring a fresh perspective and I had to admit she was smart.

"I think everyone who leads feels that way, but you didn't sound that way." She winked. "It sounded like you at least had floatation devices on your arms ... you know, not *completely* out of your depth."

I barked out a laugh and all my muscles relaxed. "Thanks."

"That's better."

We hugged one more time before we headed out to strengthen bonds, a much-needed practice

The next few hours settled my mantle in place as I took Luna around to speak to each pack member. About halfway through the circling, Conner joined us. I could almost see him watching the connections form and firm up as each person got to know Luna and him better.

After the pack left, I realized someone had made dinner. A pot of chili bubbled away on the stove and when I followed my nose into the kitchen, Dayna pulled a loaf of cornbread from the oven. "Did you make this?"

A spark of delight colored her face. "I didn't. But Julez told me when to take the cornbread from the oven. I hear you have another big meeting coming up, so we should get to eating before you faint away. I mean, that lasagna wasn't nearly enough."

Laughing, I headed to the cupboard to get a stack of bowls. Brooke and Jade followed me in. Brooke sighed. "I love living in California, but chili tastes better when there's snow on the ground."

After taking a bite, Luna smirked. "Not as good as Dad's, but it'll do."

I raised an eyebrow. "Does this mean you can do better? I mean, I'll happily have you cook some later this week."

She chuckled.

My heart pounded in my chest and my hands were cold as I sat in the office waiting to join the teleconference with all the alphas. I wasn't sure how Dad had set up this system, but despite it being online, we could talk freely here. Everything was completely locked down, giving us an ability to communicate.

Luna used the chair from earlier, sitting next to me. It would be easier if we were both on the same side of the desk. I logged into the computer and opened up the meeting app. It only took a moment for other boxes to pop up showing pairs of people. I didn't recognize everyone—I hadn't met all the alphas yet—but a warmth filled me when I saw my parents' faces.

"Hiya, Pebble, how are you treating our pack?" Dad asked. Part of me longed for him to call me 'Applesauce,' but this was the alphas meeting, and the nickname wouldn't be appropriate.

"That's a long story and I'm going to wait until everyone is here to share."

His smile tightened. "Yeah, I know. I've heard some of the rumors. Sorry this has been such a tense winter break so far. Not quite the nothing we promised."

A laugh bubbled out of me. "Not your fault." As we spoke, all the other members of the meeting logged in.

The warm smiles from José and Bevin made me feel like I was in a class and in with the popular kids ... somehow in the 'know.' I smiled back at them, returning Bevin's smirk.

"Okay, everyone," Mom said, her eyes dashing around her screen. "I think we should start with introductions. I believe River and I are the only ones here who know everyone. We should end with Pebble. I know she has a lot to share. Though you all know us, River and I are down in Tennessee. Kendall and Iris were killed in an attack over New Years. This pack is a mess. There aren't any alpha level wolves here—not even close. We came down because we had Pebble to take over in Wisconsin, as well as others who can support her."

One of the other alphas narrowed his eyes. "Do you have any new details about how two alphas could've been taken out?"

Dad nodded. "Yes, but let's finish the introductions then we'll get into those details."

An older couple smiled. The woman spoke. "Hi, I'm Cameron and this is Finley. We're from Massachusetts. Things have been quiet here."

A wide smile crossed Rory's face. He said, "Things have been quiet here in Florida." Tilly slapped his shoulder. "Oh! Sorry. Hi, I'm Rory, this is Tilly, we're from Florida. I guess there is one person we don't know. I do want to mention that Conner, our son, has relocated to the Wisconsin pack for college. We'd discussed this, but he left just after New Years. If we'd known everything that was coming, we may have waited a semester, but we'd've been wrong." His eyes widened. "Pebble, can I give this bit of information, or will it take away some of your thunder?"

Without warning, another laugh bubbled out of me. His exuberance was infectious. One of Luna's eyebrows rose. On the screen, José and Bevin smiled just as wide. "Go ahead, this is your news as much as ours. I have more to share on the topic, but I'll wait until it's my turn."

Both Floridian alphas' faces brightened with their excitement. Then Rory rubbed his hands together. "Okay, it didn't take Pebble more than a few minutes to hear Conner tell the story for her to realize our son is the second epsilon wolf in the American packs."

Shock and amusement filled the boxes, depending on whether the alphas knew or not. Though it wasn't possible, the emotions almost crossed through the computer, tickling my nose.

The only female alpha I didn't know—it had to be one of the ones from Colorado—leaned in. "A second epsilon? That's ... I don't know. Do we know how that's possible?"

Under the desk, my hands trembled, while on the screen, I tried to look calm. "If you wait, Luna and I have a theory. But we'd like to get through all the introductions

... especially since Luna doesn't know any of you. Well, she's met my parents, but that was only briefly."

Everyone paused. We hadn't told anyone about our theory, not even my parents, not even José and Bevin. I'd even asked Jade to hold off on the gossip, and it looked like she'd agreed. We'd waited until this meeting for everything so that all the packs would learn together.

The same female spoke again. "Well, in that case, my name is Colleen and this is Frank. We're from Colorado. Though we haven't met you, we did work together a few weeks ago when a couple of lone wolves attacked Pebble and Luna in our state. Heather, one of our wolves, worked with Pebble to clean up the situation, then she took these two out for dinner. There was some talk at the time about lone wolves taking back power, but the wolf we had wasn't very coherent."

Luna stiffened. Looking over at her, I saw her body was tight. She obviously remembered the attack as well as I did. It was at that point that we had learned about each other's animals and that we were connected.

"I'm José—" his soft voice filled the room, and as always released a tension I'd been holding. Of all the alphas, he and Bevin were the ones I'd most love to work with. "—and this is Bevin. We lead the new California pack. I like that we're no longer the new alphas in town." He winked at me, and I smiled in return.

I could feel Luna moving. Shifting my eyes I saw her shake her head. "That's why we're here, to give you seniority." Luna's dry humor had some of the people on the call startled, others chuckling.

José waggled his brows. "Why, thank you."

Nerves played havoc throughout my body, like squirrels darting through the trees. It was our turn, and I needed to focus. Before I spoke, Luna placed a hand on my lower back, and the squirrels quieted. Gratefully, I took a breath. "Hi, everyone. I'm Pebble Stone. I know many of you were planning on meeting me this summer—well, surprise!" I waved my hands in front of the screen. Once everyone waved back, I looked at Luna, then back at the camera. "Some of you know that I've been having premonitions my whole life. Well, one of those visions brought me to Luna. She's my co-leader here in Wisconsin."

She and I had spoken about this, if she wanted to say anything. The muscles in her arms and shoulders tensed. "Hi. I'm Luna Zweck, and I'm from Maine. I know I'm new to being a wolf and to the pack, but I'm ready to help out with what's happening here in Wisconsin."

Colleen's eyes narrowed. "And what *is* happening there?"

Luna smiled. "We have lone wolves ... or wolves trying to band together in their hate against us, and they want to take over. They started down in Tennessee and then came up here. One of their number joined our pack as a mole, but we've found her. From what we can tell, she doesn't know this, so we're going to use her to find the others."

Finley, whose voice was much lower than I'd expected, spoke next. "Do you know why this is happening? I know there's always been some tension between us and lone wolves, but is there more?"

"Yes," I said with certainty. "The person who joined our pack, she's been recognized as being part of the wolf cult that tried to take down the California group all those years ago. We have it on good authority she's one of the kids that was sent away when the Dynasty planned their attack all those year ago in California. Since they lost, we believe she and the others now want revenge. We believe that she and her cronies are coming after us in Wisconsin first because the California leaders come from here."

"Didn't they go after the Tennessee pack first? Or even us first?" Colleen asked.

I nodded as I breathed slowly. "We believe that was a tactic to draw away Mom and Dad ... Hazel and River. Wisconsin has been pretty vocal about my training. They gambled and won on which alphas would step up and take over."

It felt like Bevin looked right at me, though with the way the images of all the alphas were, I didn't think I could tell that for sure. "Do we have any information on a permanent alpha for Tennessee?" His concern could be felt, even over the computer. "From what I've heard, Pebble is doing a great job but having been an alpha in college ... it's nice to not have to do both."

"Bevin, you're skipping all around my announcements," I teased. His smile warmed me. "I'm going to jump back to the Floridian giddiness and the epsilons, if that's okay. Then I'm going to head back to Tennessee."

All around the screen, I saw confusion but agreement.

"The lone wolves have left us messages through deceased tourists and seemingly random people around our city. They also attacked a couple of my friends while we were out, and I was separated from them. I stopped them before any damage could happen." Though learning about these actions was important, in lieu of everything else, I could see some of the expressions on the alphas morph. They were ready to interrupt. *It's like they worry I'm too young and don't know how to prioritize.* "Though I'd thought both friends were norms, one ended up being an out of state child of werewolves. Moreover, one day, they'll be a third epsilon ..."

There was an uproar of talk and shock. I had to wait it out. When I looked over at Luna, she sported a smile that mirrored my own. Once the chatter slowed down, I continued. "I have a friend; their name is Fern. They're not a wolf yet, but Jade, who is here in Wisconsin, confirmed that not only will Fern be a wolf in a couple of months, they'll also be an epsilon." I paused as everyone took in this news. "Once we realized we had three epsilon wolves together, in one room, we had to figure out the how and why."

"Do we know Fern's parents?" Mom asked. I knew she wouldn't be able to stop herself.

"I do." I tried not to laugh as she narrowed her eyes at me. "If you let me finish, you'll know too." Dad chuckled, waiting for my answer. "Their dad is Ronald Meadows, and their mother is Amy Meadows." The look on their faces told me most of the people knew who I spoke of. Only José and Bevin looked blank. "The thing most of you may not know about is, Mr. Meadows was bitten at the same time Dad and Rory were. He was in college in Atlanta at the time."

There was a stillness in the images. I watched as the different people slowly made connections. Finally, Colleen asked, "Is Amy a natural wolf?"

"Yes." I nodded as I spoke. "As are Mom and Tilly. But," I held up my hands before anyone else could speak, "there is more. There is a quote in an old book of lore. It states that," I looked down at my notes, " *'Created strength mixed with natural power will bring pack balance.'*" My focus returned to the computer screen. "Those of us here in Wisconsin believe the created strength is alpha level bitten wolves. The rest is clearer. We have three mixed couples and three epsilon wolves. Jade will be training Conner and Fern remotely from California."

"And who will write the book?" Dad insisted.

Luna leaned forward. "Fern volunteered. They were warned about you."

Everyone laughed at that.

Once things calmed, I said, "Fern and I will drive to visit their dad after the full moon. We are hoping to convince him to return to Tennessee. So far he's been very resistant to all our talks."

Mom's eyebrow popped up. "He spoke to you?"

"Yes," I said, smiling wide. "He did. It wasn't very productive, but we did have a conversation." I leaned back with a sigh. "I think I've gotten through all the announcements from my corner of the world."

José chuckled. "What? That's it? As the newest alpha, we expected much more from you, Pebble." A lightness filled me at his words.

Dad said, "Well, I guess it's my turn. With some help from my experts in Wisconsin, we've compared the attack on Pebble's friends last week with the attack here. The setup was exactly the same. The lone wolves came up behind the alphas and slit their throats before they knew anything was happening. Then they were tossed down the alley to two waiting wolves, who destroyed the evidence of knife wounds with gnawing. This two-pronged attack with people attacking in human and wolf form appears to be their MO."

Cameron huffed. "So, we can't let our guard down. They kill from behind without warning. They stab a person in the back. Such awful wolves."

There wasn't much else to share in the meeting, and everyone was ready to call it done. As the others logged out, Dad asked me to stay on.

"I miss you, Dad."

His smile was sad. "I miss you too, Applesauce, but you're doing a great job. Mom and I are proud. And Luna, it sounds like you're getting adjusted there as well. You didn't have much time, and you handled yourself perfectly here."

"Thanks, Mr. Stone."

"Call me River. We're all leaders here."

Mom smiled at us both. "Enjoy your first moon run, Luna. I'm proud of you both."

Chapter 4 – Saying Goodbye

The silence in the barn seeped into my body as I began my morning routine. After the intensity of the previous day, I needed to sweat out my stress. My book listed cardio, so I ran. When I'd checked the weather on the computer—*gods, I wish I had a phone*—it was beyond too cold to run outside this morning.

I'd spent time after the alpha meeting looking for my phone, but I didn't find it. The fact that Tyler said it had been off had confirmed a lot of things for me. I rarely let my battery drop too low, so it being off meant someone had turned it off. Despite that, I'd searched the kitchen and living room, spending extra time in the areas of the couch where items were often lost in the void of sacrifices to the gods.

It was early, so no one else joined me as I let everything percolate in my head. It was nice to have some time to get all the new information, new ideas, and new feelings settled and in place in my mind.

Ever since I'd been bitten, my wolf had been giving me premonitions, visions, and a bit extra in terms of knowing the world around me. I didn't get the premonitions often, only when she had something important to tell me. If I were epsilon, she'd probably just pull me into a headspace and talk to me, but I wasn't gifted with such luxuries.

Over the last several months, I'd had some long-term and repeating visions. That was new. I wasn't sure if it was because they were about me—in the past they'd always been about other pack members—or because I'd been too thick to understand them. Either way, it felt good to not have a vision hanging over my head. There were enough other things to worry about. Maybe, at this point at least, we knew the cards dealt us.

After thirty minutes, I headed over to my book, recorded my information, and debated doing more. It was still early, and I had energy buzzing in my body, but I knew there was still a lot to do, and I didn't have time for an extra-long workout.

It was my last day with Jade and Brooke; there was a good chance my sister would wake early. A shower and coffee and the hope of time with Jade pulled me back to the house. In the kitchen, the stillness from the barn continued to resonate. Everyone continued to sleep. I set up the coffee maker, then headed to my room to get a change of clothes and to shower.

In the shower, I let the warm water beat down on my sore muscles. Eyes closed, I tuned in to where I had the connections to the pack blocked off behind a sturdy fence. As I mentally checked in with the different pack members, or the impressions I had of them, I knew many of them also slept. A few were up, the stress of the Monday morning a slight pressure on their connection. Others were awake and relaxed, maybe reading or watching TV. Maybe they were already drinking a morning coffee or tea.

If I spend a bit of time thinking about this, I could almost assign colors to their states. I'll have to think about this. I wonder if my parents or any of the other alphas do something like that.

Back in my room, I put on jeans and a shirt with a rhinoceros on it which read, *Protect the Chubby Unicorn.*

Heading to the kitchen, I heard Jade talking in the living room. As I passed through, I saw she was in there with Conner and Fern. I didn't tune in as I went for coffee, then I swung back to sit in a recliner.

Conner's brow furrowed. "So, you can talk to any of your pack ... mentally?"

Sighing dramatically, Jade looked at me. "Pebble, you're his alpha. Can you do the demo?"

I wasn't sure if the other two had heard me come in. With my legs curled under me and my hands hugging my coffee, I raised an eyebrow to her. "You want me to initiate?"

"Why not? You've done it enough, you know what to do."

There was a tension in the air as Conner gaped at me. I closed my eyes and imagined a door. In the past the door always had a feel of Jade. I wasn't sure how to explain it—it just was the door to her. I imbued this door with the feeling of Conner. I didn't know him as well, so I hoped it worked. Lifting a mental fist, I knocked.

"Ah, Jade. Why do I hear a tapping in my head?" Conner's minty confusion filled the room.

With a gentle voice, Jade guided Conner through what he was experiencing. It didn't take long for me to hear him in my head. *"Um, I don't know if I'm just talking to myself, and if I am, I guess it isn't too weird, because don't we do that all the time? Heh."* He sounded confused and a bit awed. *"But, um, this is Conner. Am I talking to Pebble?"*

A small smile tugged at my lips. *"Nope, not Pebble. I am the voice in your head. And you're learning the ways of the crazy one."* He gaped at me. I smiled wide then sipped my coffee. *"Yes, silly, you did it. You figured this out, my friend. It takes energy so you'll need extra food. I think it causes headaches as well. You'll want to be careful.*

Oh! And ask Jade about power sharing. So many things! Take notes."

As I savored my morning elixir, he snapped his head to her. "You can share power? What does that even mean?"

In her seat, Jade slumped. "Too much information, Pebble. I was hoping to trickle things out slowly. Like a proper class with lessons and a curriculum. No more jumping ahead, okay?"

"I guess." With a large sigh, I leaned back. "If you say so, sis." I winked at her.

She continued explaining things to Conner and Fern. For the most part, Fern just wrote furiously in a notebook, though my friend's attention appeared to be complete. Eventually I got up to make breakfast. It was all interesting, but I knew the topic well. Conner was going to need food.

I put a bagel in the toaster. Once mine popped, I started toasting them for the trio in the living room. Dayna and Brooke sauntered in and began making their breakfast. After bringing a tray into the living room, I joined the other two at the kitchen table. The three of us sat in silence, drinking coffee, eating food, and listening to the conversation from the other room. Once they finished, the other three joined us, both Conner and Fern smiling wide.

Fern sat down next to me after getting their own drink. "Your sister knows everything. It's amazing. Like, I thought you were smart, but she can answer every question either of us threw at her."

"Gods above, she's going to be awful for months after hearing that." Brooke hit her head against her hand a few times. "You know Jade only seems wise because she's so old, right?"

Sitting down next to Brooke and giving her a kiss, Jade laughed. "I wouldn't be so quick to throw that word around, wife."

With narrowed eyes, Brooke shook her head. "I would stop that sentence right there ... assuming you want to share my bed when we get home."

"Speaking of," I said loudly, wanting to cut off that conversation. "When does your plane leave? How much time do I get with the two of you?"

Dayna went to the pantry and took out more cereal. "Aw, I was hoping you two were staying longer. You have to leave so soon? It's only been a couple of days."

"Our plane leaves at noon, so we need to start packing up." Jade smiled at Dayna. "And we'd love to stay longer, even join you for your run tomorrow, but there are a few reasons it'd be a bad idea." Her head snapped to Luna, who chose that moment to join us. "First of all, with three new wolves, and this being Pebble's *and* Luna's first moon run as alphas, they don't need extras out for the night. Second," she reached over to clasp Brooke's hand, "I miss our babies."

"I'm surprised we got you for as long as we did," I admitted. "It's been really good having you here. We'd adjust if you could stay, but I understand why leaving is probably for the best."

The morning slipped by. The only other interesting thing that happened was Tyler bringing me a burner phone. "I saved some of the pack numbers onto the phone. If we can't get yours back in a couple of days, I'll send a kill command and get you a new one."

"Thanks, Tyler. So, this has all the pack numbers, or just you, Tanner, and Clare?"

"It has your parents and a few others. Maybe half the pack. It was a list your dad had set up for emergency phones."

"Okay, sounds good."

All too soon I had to drive Jade and Brooke to the airport. I tried not to get misty, but, although Jade was still here, I already missed her. "I really wish you could stay."

"You have this, Pebble. You're doing great." Jade squeezed my knee in support. "We're all so proud of you."

"I know. I just ... it's so much. I can't believe those creeps are still harassing all of us."

Jade rubbed my leg. "I know. It'll all be over before you know it. Then you'll have your pack and your friends. School will be a breeze ... or as much as classes and college can be. Just hang in there, sis."

With a big sigh, I wiped my eyes and pulled up to the drop-off lane at the airport. "I love you, Jade. You, too, Brooke. Thank you both for coming."

Getting out of the car, I gave them both hugs. While Jade's hug was that of family, sister, and home, Brooke's also brought the touch of submissive wolf and a needed break in my emotional turmoil. She whispered, "You really are incredible, Pebble. Everyone in California is amazed by how strong you are. You have all our support."

The drive home was quick. When I walked into the living room, Fern sat there alone on a couch. "The others went downtown for sushi. I figured I'd wait and see what you wanted for lunch."

"You don't think we'll get sick of each other driving to visit your dad?"

"Nah. So, Mexican?" They waggled their brows.

I sat next to them. "Sounds good. I always enjoy a good burrito."

"Okay, one more thing." Fern pulled out their phone. "I got a text from Hollis. She wants us to come over tomorrow morning." They scrunched up their nose. "I don't know. I want to be excited, but I'm worried."

Reaching over, I clasped Fern's hand. Whereas part of me cried out in terror at the idea of losing my best friend, that thought would break me right now ... it was too much. There were so many things to worry about, I couldn't add to my list. I refused to put the cart before the horse. "I wouldn't sweat it. It's Hollis."

Chapter 5 – Running From Emotions

The drive to Hollis's house was quick, as always. Despite that, my emotions morphed from calm to near panic in the few blocks. Luckily, Fern wasn't a wolf yet and couldn't smell emotions. I'd learned how to mask what I felt behind a calm, blank face, so I hoped they couldn't tell.

After I parked, we sat for a minute. It was the last few seconds before we'd learn the truth about what Hollis was thinking. Breathing slowly through my nose, I worked to unclench my jaw. At the end of the day, the thought of losing my best friend scared me to my core.

What will I do if Hollis wants to cut off our friendship? She's been a rock to me for years, a connection to the world outside my pack. She was the one thing separate from being a wolf that made sense. She's probably a big part of why I survived being turned so young. Without her, I don't know if I can maintain my humanity as well ... I don't want to slip into being only a pack wolf, not at my age. On my own, I would've been alone and socially awkward throughout my school years. She taught me who I wanted to be when my siblings left. Not to mention, without Hollis, the rest of college ... gods, I don't want to think about it.

"You ready?" Fern's gentle voice pulled me from my thoughts. Their hand on my arm warmed a chill I hadn't realized had started.

"Yeah, it's time." My voice came out small and breathy. With a bit of effort I squeezed my hands together, letting my nails bite into my palms. "I mean, yes, let's go."

We headed up to the house. As always, there were two cars in the driveway we had to navigate around. At the door, Fern rang the bell. They gave me a sad smile. "When I arrived, Hollis and her parents told me I could come right in, I didn't have to knock. Now I don't feel right doing that."

I smiled tightly. "Yeah, I get it. You haven't been here long, but things have changed so much so quickly."

"Yeah, I thought I knew what was going on in my life and with my friends, but I know ... give me a few months and then my life will really change." A smile lit their face. "Then you won't be able to stop me."

The door opened and Hollis stood there, eyes red, face blotchy, wearing pajamas and her hair disheveled. "Follow me."

She turned and lumbered across the living room to the hallway to her bedroom. As I followed, I noticed that neither of her parents were around. An earthy, defeated scent wafted from her, filling the space until we got into her space.

Hollis had a nice room with a queen-sized bed, a desk, a dresser, and a closet. When my parents let me redecorate, she convinced her parents to let us redo her area as well. We found paint colors and spent one summer day painting her walls a sky blue. Her desk had been white and pink with hearts, so we went over it in navy blue and trimmed it out in the same lighter blue as the walls.

Since the only option was paint, her bedding was all the same as when she'd been younger. The current set was yellow with small white flowers. We'd debated getting clothing dye, but in the end, we decided to stop with home decorating and move on to our next adventure ... rock climbing.

Currently, there was a combination of scents swirling around us. Defeat, sadness, and regret. All of those were different timbers of earth, from soil to trees. But interweaving these, a sour stress that tickled my nose. The potpourri of Hollis's emotions didn't bode well for the next few minutes.

Hollis sat at the desk. "The two of you can sit on the bed. Otherwise, someone would need to sit on the floor."

Fern and I sat. My heart hurt for my friend. I was so worried for her. "How are you doing, Hollis? Is there anything we can do? Any questions we can answer?"

Hollis's face tightened. It looked like she was about to cry but held it back. "I'm fine ... no, I'm not fine, but—" She shook her head. "Look, I know in my head, logically, that you weren't trying to keep things from me, that the secrets you kept were for a reason, but Pebble, my heart can't reconcile it."

A hand tightened in my chest. My heart was breaking. Breathing became hard. "What are you saying?"

Fern put a hand on my leg and my vision, which I hadn't realized had been darkening, cleared.

Hollis's eyes snapped to the connection, and she frowned. Before either of us could say anything, Fern sighed. "This isn't what you're thinking. It's a werewolf thing. Pebble was spinning out of control ... emotionally. She needed the touch of pack, that's it. Believe me, if I could choose, I would come back here, Hollis, spend my remaining days with you."

"No." Hollis shook her head. "I can't. I need time away from both of you, at least for a little more time."

"What about when school starts up?" There was a quaver in my voice that I tried to hide. I didn't want her to know how much the question worried me.

Hollis turned her back to us, facing her desk. "I'm going to ask for a change of dorms ... a new roommate."

A wave of sadness washed through me. I covered my face with my hands trying to hold in my feelings. "Don't. I'll live at home. I'm probably going to be needed there anyway. You can stay in the dorms, in our room. No reason to upset things." I let my hands drop as my words blanketed the area.

She sniffled and turned around. "You'd do that? Move out of the dorms and commute?"

"Hollis, you're my best friend, I'd do almost anything for you. Just ask and ... yes, I'd do that for you."

She gave me a small smile. "Anything but tell me the truth."

A dagger to the heart would've hurt less. "I've told you most things. There is only one secret I kept from you. And that was because I couldn't tell you."

"But you'll move out?"

"If that's really what you want. I'll stay away. I'm still hoping one day you'll decide our friendship is worth it. Maybe one day you'll want to meet the pack, learn more about the wolves. I don't want to take that from you." I bit my lip. "Now that you know, there's no more secrets. You can ask me anything."

Hollis flinched as if she'd been hit. "I don't think so. You can keep stuff in the dorms for now, but if it gets to be too much, I'm going to transfer."

"That's fair. But I promise to give you space, if that's what you need."

Next to me, I could feel Fern trembling. "What about me?"

Before Fern finished their words, Hollis shook her head. "I just ... I can't. Not yet. I need you both to give me space."

There wasn't much more to say, so we both got up to leave. I wanted to give Hollis a hug but knew that wouldn't be well received.

Out in the car, I sat for a moment and let my emotions race through me. Clasping the steering wheel, my knuckles turned white, and I howled my pain and sadness. I knew I should be better, hold my emotions in until I was alone, but I couldn't. I was just so mad. I was angry at the wolves that outed us, at Hollis for being unwilling to bend on something I couldn't change about myself, and my parents, my stupid birth parents, that did this to me all those years ago.

The heat of my tears warmed my cheeks.

Back at pack house, the wolves would be able to scent my mood. I wanted to get myself under control before I got there.

Fern put a hand on my shoulder. "It'll be okay, Pebble, just give her time."

"Yeah, I know, time. I just ... she's always been in my corner. I'd like to be there for her now, but I'm the cause of her misery. I can't be both the problem and the shoulder for her to cry on." My words came out rough around my tears.

"Just give her time." They repeated, leaning over to give me the hug I so desperately needed. I returned it just as tightly.

Closing my eyes, I leaned my head back and did something I'd never done before. *Sonnara, God of sun and that which helps me keep my humanity, please help Hollis to find her way back to me. I'll do anything, give up anything, just ... don't take her away from me.*

Fern and I drove around for a half-hour before we headed back to the pack den. By then, I felt centered and calm. There were a smattering of cars in the driveway. It was the night of the full moon and those people who didn't have nine to five jobs were getting ready early.

Inside the house, there were people gathered in the living room and kitchen. The scent of food cooking made my stomach cheer.

I went to sit next to Piper and Julez. Julez had a smirk on her face. The scent of jasmine oozed from her as she sat proud. I slouched, knowing where this was going. "What?"

"I knew she was no good." It felt like a punch to the gut, and after my morning with Hollis, I wasn't sure how much more I could take. With an effort, I forced myself into a different headspace, forcing a layer of tranquility on myself until I wasn't surrounded by wolves.

My head swung around the room to determine who all could overhear us. "Shush. First of all, we're keeping this on the downlow. How the hell do you even know? Second of all, I have no idea what you're talking about."

The other woman shook her head. "You have an awful poker face, did you know that?"

I just waved my hand in a circular motion, waiting for her to continue.

"Fine. I called Estrella to complain about her, because someone in a store had a similar attitude and it was annoying. I told Estrella I didn't want to have to deal with *that* on a moon night, because I think of the full moon run as being relaxing and *our nights*. Not nights of dealing with people treating our child poorly. Anyway, she said I couldn't tell anyone, but you're the alpha, so you already know."

With a groan, I rubbed my forehead. *And this is why secrets don't get kept in the pack. I'll have to speak with Clare.*

"Okay, well, do a better job than either Clare or Estrella at keeping this a secret. Apparently the pack has forgotten how to not spread top-secret gossip." I knew I snapped, but my emotions were frayed.

Julez continued to smirk.

Aunt Allison came over to me and took my hands. "I'm not sure what's up, but we need to talk." Her eyes narrowed. "Julez."

I shivered. She was usually nicer, but she could obviously feel my turmoil. No headspace could hide my emotions from a submissive wolf.

We headed towards the hall with the meeting room. "Talk to me. Why the emotions? They've been on a roller coaster all day. I debated calling, but figured we'd be together tonight, and I could see your face as we spoke."

Her hands on my arms brought me peace, at last. In as few words as I could, I explained what happened with Hollis. With every fiber in my body, I worked to not cry. Aunt Allison pulled me into a tight hug, an almost yellow glow emanating from around her. "Sweetheart, I'm so sorry. She's been your rock for so long. I'm sure she'll come around. Give it time. I know this last week or so has felt like a lifetime, but emotions will fall back into place."

I sighed and relaxed, shivering as it felt like pieces of me that had been misaligned readjusted.

"That's better. You told your new wolves about using us," she tapped my nose, "but you seem to have forgotten about us submissives yourself. Now, go be amazing."

Before I could do more than turn towards the living room, the front door opened, and Tanner came in. "Pebble, can we talk?" Though he walked with purpose, there was a small smile on his face, and he headed for the kitchen, not anywhere private.

Happy for the excuse to not return to Julez, followed him into the kitchen. "What's up?"

"Well, I was thinking. Since Luna has accepted her role as alpha, I think you should alleviate some of the pressure—" he tapped my head.

Thinking about it, I looked over to where Luna sat with Dayna and Conner in the dining room. "You think I should give some of the pack to her?"

"Yes, I'm tired of being in that crowded brain of yours. And, I think, like your mom, you shouldn't hold close family." My grin matched his. I knew he couldn't actually feel how many wolves were linked to me, only a vague impression of the direction his alpha was relative to him, but the idea was humorous.

"Aunt Allison and Uncle Jackson?"

The side of his mouth twitched. "I'm glad we agree."

I groaned at the thought of explaining this to Luna and what her reaction would be, but I knew the outcome would be for the best. "Fine, I'll go talk with her."

His smile grew as he grabbed a banana and headed into the living room.

In the dining room, I sat down across from Luna. The others all looked at me. "Luna, are you ready for one more piece of the alpha puzzle?"

Her face scrunched up in a sneer. *There's the Luna I've come to love ... er, know.* "To be a pack, the alphas hold the members in their head. Most are in one alpha, but a few go to the second. Maybe eighty-twenty."

"What does that mean 'hold in their head'? Is this some weird telepathy thing?"

"It's an emotional connection mostly. I can sense when someone in the pack needs me. To some extent, I know where a pack member is. It isn't a lot of information, but it's what connects us ... you know, makes us pack."

Luna's face tightened. "And you think I should take a few of the pack?"

"Yes." I threw up my hands and smiled. "Not too many, but maybe three or four."

"Who?" she asked, eyes narrowing.

We continued talking for a few minutes, discussing who, what it would feel like, and how it would be achieved. In the end, Dayna requested to be on the Luna list. Despite being family, they hadn't grown up together and I saw no reason to say no.

The wolves didn't have to be there for the transfer to happen, but we decided to call them in, so they knew what we were doing. Before the moon run, Luna had four wolves in her head: Aunt Allison, Uncle Jackson, Tanner, and Dayna. She adjusted to their presence faster than me, but four was an easier number than I got when my parents left for Tennessee.

Easton and Piper's mom, Helen, made a Mediterranean fish and rice dish. Everyone sat and ate and then we headed out to shift.

The new wolves shifted faster, and Tanner and I were ready for Luna and Dayna's attacks. It was possible they'd do it one or two more times.

Though we'd run together after the first pack meeting, this was a moon run, and we had Mondara's power, the moon god, surging through us as we ran and worshiped her.

As the pack took to the woods, I could feel the groups' energy pulse through and around me. My connection to Luna was the strongest. For the first hour, we practically flew, the snow crunching under our paws, the wind combing our fur, and the link of the wolves as we howled our song, heady. The elation became an energy surrounding us, guiding us, and pushing us forward.

Part of my personal melody, my howls, were cries to Mondara, asking her to fix the fissure between me and Hollis. In this form, the rest of my family may have heard the sorrow in my cries but would think my emotions were for my parents and their need to leave us all behind, abandon their pack for another. A call to my god for strength for all the changes in my life. They weren't wrong, but part of my sorrow belonged to my friend and the loss to my link to humanity.

Eventually, I sensed a deer on the wind. With the instinct of the animal, I began orchestrating the movements of the group. Some would herd the deer, wearing it down. Others would run with me, ready to attack.

Plan in place, we split up.

Everyone danced in perfect harmony, the play perfectly arranged in my mind.

Next to me, Tanner and Luna leapt a fallen tree. To our right, I could feel Clare, Estrella, and Easton on the other side of the deer.

Within my soul, I could feel when the deer began to falter. Bunching my muscles, I leapt, flying through the air, and landing on the neck. Around me, the others joined in, and in quick order the deer was down.

Luna and I each took our fill, then backed up. She rubbed up against me, a joy permeating from her. The mantle fully settled over her as we watched our pack finally become ours.

A light rainbow of colors seemed to emanate from the mass of wolves. As I squinted, I realized each individual wolf slightly glowed a different color. Though I'd been seeing the colors before, they suddenly became more ... brighter, bigger, more intense.

What is going on? Is this something else my parents didn't warn me about?

Chapter 6 – Life In Technicolor

I sat in the kitchen, drinking coffee, and eating sausage, eggs, and toast with a side of sliced apples. The run the night before settled something deep inside me, joining me more completely with the members of the pack, even the ones linked in Luna's mind. I finally felt like the alpha of the Wisconsin pack.

The echoes I had in my head were less somehow. I could still feel them, but they weren't as intense. They felt less like bees and more like something manageable. They were also more unique. I could focus on each individual and know who it was without as much chaos.

The one thing I didn't understand, I hadn't expected, were the strange colors emanating from the different people in the kitchen. When I tried to ask my wolf about it, she was oddly mute. There was nothing there to tell me what was going on.

It was early. I knew I had to wait to call even Mom, though she was probably up, to ask her what was going on. I could text, but she didn't know my new number.

As always, when I had come in from the run, Helen was up early preparing coffee and food. There was a slight purple glow shining from around her. I'd rubbed my eyes, but the haze around her didn't shift. I stumbled, confused, to the shower, but once I'd dressed and returned to the kitchen, the color was still there, though there seemed to be a bit of orange mixed in as well. The two hues swirled around her like a dim light show. It wasn't flashy, but it was there.

The next few wolves that woke, dressed, and came in, were people who needed to get to work. Fred, Janet, Greg, Monica, Andy, Chris. Each of them were smudged with their own light show. Fred and Janet were blue, though Janet had a bit of orange swirling around her. Greg, like Helen was purple, though he had some light green mixed in.

I started to think the shades were based on couples. But then Andy came in an indigo swirled with yellow followed by Chris a very clear green ... just shades of green.

Aunt Allison and Uncle Jackson came in, yellow and green respectfully, but they had a white glow connecting them.

I rubbed my eyes, wondering if I'd hurt my brain somewhere along the line.

"Hello, Pebble, you there?"

My head jerked up, and I gazed at Helen. "What? I'm sorry, I'm a bit ... um, distracted." I lifted my mug, but it was empty. A groan escaped me as I put it down.

"I can tell, dear, you've been staring at everyone mumbling all morning. Can I get you more coffee?" Helen was like everyone's mother, warm and caring.

The buzz in the room covered the scatteredness of my reaction to her. "Yes, please."

When she returned, Helen sat to my left, focusing on the table and those sitting near me, I realized Luna, Dayna, Conner, and Fern had joined me as well. Just like everyone else, they had their own glowing colors. My head felt like it would split open if the light show didn't end.

I lifted the mug. "Thanks, I really need this this morning."

Helen reached out and rubbed my arm. "Can you tell me what's wrong? If I didn't know better I'd say you were coming down with something."

In her day-to-day life, Helen was a nurse. If wolves didn't heal so well, she'd be utilized full time helping to care for us.

I shot Luna a quick look, then faced Helen. "I don't know. For all I know, this is more alpha secret stuff. My parents left so fast, I fear there were a ton of things they never told me."

"Pebble, there are secrets and there is a girl who looks like she's seen a ghost. We'll call this nurse-patient privilege. Tell me what's wrong."

My head fell back as I thought about the implications of her words. I finally decided I needed to talk to someone. "Have you ever heard of a brain issue where someone suddenly saw ... I don't know, colored glows around other people?"

One of Helen's eyebrows popped up. "Colorful glows? Like, the people in the room look like ghosts?"

I huffed out a gust of air, knowing I sounded like a fool. "No, it isn't like that. It looks like ... gah! I don't know. Like everyone has a light just behind them and I can see just a haze of it all around their body. Some people have a swirl of two tinted light surrounding them."

On my other side, Luna barked out a laugh. "You sound like my mom and her auras. *'Everyone is ringed in shades defining them, Luna. If you can read their individual hues, you'll know a bit about them. The better you get at reading the auras, the more you'll know about them.'*"

A groan escaped me as I rubbed my face. "Auras? But that's a goose ability and I'm not a goose, you are."

Dayna started to laugh. "But you two are connected and starting to share abilities, right? Luna saw part of one of your premonitions. And now you have the aura sight she's ignored her whole life."

The words hit me like a hammer, and I slumped. "Is there any way to turn this off?" I rubbed my eyes with the heels of my hands. "Can I ignore this too until it goes away?"

"We can call my mom, but I don't think so, you just … adjust and get used to it." Luna shrugged. "I never actually ignored it. I just never saw the colors." She winked. "My skepticism kept the crazy at bay."

Helen rubbed my back. "It seems like you have everything figured out. I'm glad." She got up and headed back into the rainbow crowd of the kitchen.

Now that I knew what was going on, I avoided looking at the people in the room and quickly finished eating breakfast. "Luna, can we call your mom now?"

With all the people in the house, we headed up to the office. Luna texted her mom to ask if she'd be willing to Facetime with us.

It felt like the woman responded before Luna even sent the message.

"Luna! Last night was a full moon. How are you feeling about your decision? Have you decided to come home?" There was a tension in her voice as if she worried her daughter would make the wrong choice.

"Mom. Listen. We have a question."

"I just want to know about your life, Luna, and what is happening right now. Is that so much to ask for?"

"Last night was … it was good. I felt the pack and my connection with both them and the moon. I don't know if I can describe it, but it felt right. Now, Mom, we have a question ... maybe a situation." Luna spoke quickly, as if trying to get through her observations before her mom could ask more. Despite the words, the vanilla scent of delight permeated the air as she spoke.

Her mom smiled. "I'm really glad to hear that this was the right move. I knew you'd get there in the end. You really are my daughter ... the right mix of brain and intuition. Imagining you leading all those wolves will make me sleep better." She held up her hands. "Now, what's your question?"

I quickly explained what happened during the run and this morning. Then, after a thought, added in what I'd been seeing over the previous week. It hadn't been as much or as intense, but it had come up.

"Tell me about the hues and shades, dear."

Not wanting to mess anything up, I shut my eyes and slowly described everything I'd seen, from the glow around my dad—gods! just over a week ago?—to the over-abundance of colors this morning.

Once I'd told her everything I remembered, she smirked, looking exactly like her daughter. "Gods, I've been waiting for someone to discuss this all with. I don't know how it happened, but you've inherited the goose aura reading."

Head pounding, my jaw dropped. "But wait, no. That's not possible."

"It's as much a mystery to me as you, but obviously there's something in the mating bond between you and my daughter. We really should start taking notes. I don't know that there's ever been a bond between different animals, much less a were and a shifter. You should make sure you get this all down."

I couldn't believe how much she sounded like Dad. I wanted to scream. More things to add to my list. *Good thing it wasn't very big.* My head started to pound. "Can I turn it off? Or, if not, is there a book I can read?"

"Oh, no, not at all. You'll call me each morning at nine Central Standard until school starts. I believe that should give us the time we need to get you enough information to be able to interpret and control what you're seeing."

"Call or Facetime?"

"Call is enough. This is information gathering; we don't need to see each other. If we do need visuals, we'll plan it the day before. Now, I'm sure you're both tired. We'll do today's lesson at two."

Before I could say anything, she hung up.

I gaped at the blank screen. "I'm leaving on a road trip tomorrow."

Luna shrugged. "Well, call my mom at nine. You heard her."

"And if I don't?"

Amusement dripped from Luna. "You really don't want to know."

Chapter 7 – Home Sweet Home

The drive from pack house to Fern's place would take about seven hours. Fern and I decided to leave just after eight in the morning, figuring we'd arrive in time for dinner. I rose early, got in a full set in the barn, not knowing when I'd have time to do that again in the next few days, had breakfast, then packed the car. Fern knew about my lessons with Luna's mom, so they drove the first leg of the trip.

I used hands free earbuds during the lesson so Serena, Luna's mom, wouldn't hear the sounds of the car and driving.

"Yesterday, I told you about the basic rundown of the colors." Her voice was calm and surprisingly not condescending. "Did you complete the homework? Can you give me a one-word summary of each?"

The heat had finally warmed up the interior of the car and we'd made it to the interstate. There weren't many cars on the road, so I could focus on the lesson and not much else. The notebook I'd written in sat on my lap. "Going in rainbow order, as you explained it yesterday ... red would be independent, orange considerate, yellow confident, green loving, blue insightful, purple intuitive, and indigo empathic."

"Interesting. Why 'loving' for green? When we discussed it yesterday, some of the words used were social, communicator, someone who is nurturing."

My gaze fell on the trees streaming by the window as I thought about her question. "In the end, I didn't just use the information from our talk. I'm majoring in psychology and debated digging through some of my course books but thought that may give me too much to start with. So, I decided to list out the pack members I remembered who had aspects of the colors."

As I explained my process, I squeezed my eyes shut, trying to block out the extra input of the road and other cars. Then I focused on the memory of the cacophony of the rainbow of hues the morning after the run. "I know most people had more than one shade, but it felt like there was a base tone and then another color that swirled through the mist that clung to them. I don't know if that makes any sense at all. I made a chart. I used the light tint at their base to help me." My fingers tapped on my leg as I tried to sort my words into something coherent. "There was Chris, he's a submissive wolf, always supportive of everyone, Dayna who has never not been there for everyone, Conner, my Uncle Jackson, my sister. I don't know, when I looked at the list and tried to think of one word ... loving seemed to fit."

"Is that what you did for the others?" Serena sounded intrigued.

"Yeah, was that the wrong way?"

"No, not at all." There was a pause. I tried to hear what she did on the other end of the line, but nothing came through. "We try to let each learner get a feel for the auras in their own way. Using the people you know to help guide you is as valid as any other approach. Many goslings are young when they start learning about auras and understanding the people around them to this level would be beyond them."

"But people have more than one tone swirling around them, and the speed of the pigment can be dizzying." Though I'd gotten this weird ability from Luna, I wanted confirmation my version wasn't altered and different than what Serena knew.

Serena made a small sound of acknowledgement. "Tell me what you see with the people around you."

I'd warned Fern that this would happen, so they'd be ready for me to describe their aura. The last thing I wanted was to surprise or upset them while they were driving. "Okay, I'm going to use Fern, since they're the closest person to me." A smile tugged on the sides of their mouth. "Tight to their body is a blue haze, so to speak. So, they are insightful, in a word." Fern's smile grew.

"Good, now, are there any other hues?" It was almost like I could see Serena's eyes narrow as she challenged me.

"A turquoise is swirling through the blue, slow and steady." *Is there more? An orange? Is that yellow?*

"The base tint explains who that person is. For the most part the shade will always be the same. But, as people change, that can change as well. A leader who falls from grace. A positive person who turns sour. A loner who finds their people. On a day-to-day basis, your base color will be who and what you are."

"That makes sense." I continued to take notes, though it wasn't as easy in the car. "That's why I always saw my dad as red."

"Yes. As soon as Luna became a wolf and you two started to bond, a bit of this trickled down to you. That too, is common with geese. Within our gaggle we know to watch for the kids who talk about the colorful people. Not all geese can see auras, and not everyone can do it to all levels."

"So some can't see more than the base smudge?"

Serena laughed. "That's right. And others can see a secondary pigment but can't see true mates."

My hands stilled. We hadn't spoken about that. "True mates? How can you tell true mates? You mentioned you knew with me and Luna, and I forgot."

"Before I tell you, have you left anything out? Any hues or tones, any connections, any anything? As your instructor, Pebble, you need to tell me everything you see so I know how to train you properly. There are levels of aura-readers. We're just starting, doing what just about anyone would do, but soon the lessons will change."

I thought back to the kitchen and all the wolves who'd come in and out that morning. "I know I saw colors. There may have been ... well, right now I may see orange or yellow as well as the turquoise on Fern."

"Anything else?" Serena pushed.

My face scrunched up as I thought of each person in the pack. Then I wanted to kick myself since I had a list in front of me. I slowly went through the names I'd written down in the notebook. "Oh, wait, yeah, there was one other thing." My finger tapped on one name.

"Oh? And what was that?" She sounded surprisingly not frustrated with me.

"My Aunt Allison and Uncle Jackson. When they came through the kitchen. There was a white ... I don't know, like a glow, that connected them. It was faint, and only there when they were close. When they got more than a few feet apart, it dissipated. At first I thought my mind had made it up. But later when they hugged goodbye, I saw it again."

A low chuckle came over the line. Then I heard some tapping. Finally, Serena said, "Well, this is excellent. Did you know that your aunt and uncle were true mates?"

A smile spread across my face, and I warmed thinking about them. "I did."

"Well, then, now you know how I knew about you and Luna."

"But ... I've never seen that with the two of us."

"Have you looked while standing in front of a mirror? It's really the only way to read your own aura."

My mouth dropped open.

We spent the next half-hour discussing the secondary pigments and what they meant. There were a lot, but she promised to email a visual. There wasn't a great one for the base auras, a lot of that was interpretation by the practitioner. But the secondary ones, those that shifted with the mood of the person, were easier to define.

Leaning back, I rubbed my face with a groan.

Fern chuckled. "That seemed to go well."

"I can't believe how complicated this is. It's not just a simple aura."

"Pebble, we're talking about human emotions and intent. What made you think it would be easy?"

I laughed.

We were surrounded by snowy farms. Come spring and summer, the majority of them would be corn, though some would be devoted to soybeans and other common crops. "Do you want me to take over driving before we get to Illinois? So far, the traffic has been calm, but it'll get busy south of Beloit."

Fern passed a semi and sighed. "To be honest, I don't drive a lot. My parents have newer cars and are paranoid I'd get a scratch in one of them. And now that I'm living in Wisconsin, my behind the wheel has diminished even more. The thought of navigating through Chicago is a bit terrifying."

"Then we have a plan."

Just over the border into Illinois, Fern took the first exit. We gassed up the car and bought pizza. I tried not to notice the cacophony of colors shimmering around all the people near us. Though I was starting to understand, I didn't know these people and didn't feel the need to try to interpret who they were or attempt to decipher their intentions.

Back on the road, Fern pulled out their phone. "Okay, I found a video on auras and how to read and interpret them. It may be way off, but it couldn't hurt, right?"

I groaned. "I just spent an hour listening to Serena blab on about it. You want me to do *more*?"

"Well, kind of. First of all, I didn't hear any of it, and I'm interested. Second of all, she's one person. She may be an excellent teacher, but getting a second perspective can't be all that bad. And third—this is the big one—school starts soon. The more you know now, the sooner those lessons will end."

After scrunching up my face at them, I stuck out my tongue for good measure. "Fine, play the video, but I can't watch."

"I know, but it's more of a lecture, so you don't need to see anything, just listen."

Whoever created the video had similar information to the geese. He spoke in engaging, yet soothing tones, and the information was succinct and complete. Every now and then, Fern paused the phone. "Is this accurate?"

"Sounds like it."

"Good." Then they'd continue to play.

The video was one in a series. We were on the fifth, and past Chicago, when the car went silent. "Darn it, my phone died."

"Really? How low was your battery?"

"Not that low. We've been beating on the thing for almost two hours. Remember, this is video, too." Fern shook their head and snorted.

"Where's your charger?"

Fern's face scrunched up, but then they chuckled. "In my bag in the trunk, where it's safe and I won't forget it. It's fine." They waved their hand. "I can charge it later. Not to mention, you're probably at full saturation by now. I have the name of that person. I'll send it to you once I have access again. And if anyone needs to get a hold of us, they'll call you."

One of my brows popped up. "What about your dad?"

"He has the number to that phone Tyler got you. When my phone goes to voicemail, he'll call that one ... assuming he has any reason to call. I doubt he will. He knows when we're expected. I can't see him wanting to speak with us before then."

"We could continue to study auras on my phone."

"And chance killing a second phone battery? No way. We need one point of contact working. And again, you need some down time."

Despite Chicago traffic being a bear—*was that why they named their sports team that?*—the lessons helped. Then we had Indiana to drive through. Once past the interest of city roads, I had to face the endless flat fields of the state. The drive ended up being longer than planned and we arrived at Fern's place just before five.

We grabbed our bags and headed in. The scent of roasting chicken and vegetables wrapped around us like an embracing blanket. I groaned at the aroma.

"Fern! Is that you?" A gruff voice, so at odds with the welcoming scent, called from the depths of the house.

"Yes, Dad." Fern led the way into a mudroom. We dropped our bags, divested ourselves of our coats and shoes, then headed into the main house.

Fern's parents sat in the living room. Their dad looked just like Fern with short sandy hair and gray eyes. A purple haze clung to him ... intuitive. It surprised me. I had expected red or yellow. So much for my knowing what was what. He did have a blue intertwined with the purple. Despite inviting me to his home, he disapproved of my being there. Or maybe it was the overall situation. I wanted to rub my temples. I felt so overwhelmed with everything.

Their mom had blond hair, blue eyes, and an indigo aura. Her hazy glow was laced with an orangey yellow, one Fern had sported almost the whole end of the ride down. Fern's mom was optimistic about this visit. She stood and hugged Fern.

Their mom came over to me. "Hi, I'm Amy. Welcome to our home."

"Hi, Amy, I'm Pebble. Thank you for letting me come. Can I say it smells amazing?" I nearly swooned.

A smile spread across her face. "Chicken pot pie is one of Fern's favorites. I know you two are planning on staying a couple of nights, but I thought Fern may want to take you out to some of their favorite haunts tomorrow night."

Fern's dad shook my hand. "Welcome to Kentucky, alpha. Let's go sit, eat, and talk."

Not finding anything wrong with his plan, I followed him into the kitchen where the table was set.

Fern helped Amy to bring a tray of individual chicken pot pies to the table. There was already a big salad bowl. Fern looked at me. "Coffee or soda?"

"Whatever is easier." I didn't smell any made coffee. "Soda works."

Once we all had our food, I decided to get the conversation started. "Mr. Meadows—"

"Ronald."

The gruffness in his voice held some warmth. I smiled with a slight nod. "Okay, Ronald, but only if you call me Pebble." He gave me a crooked smile. "When my sister became a wolf a dozen or so years ago, word flew in the werewolf circles about her being an epsilon wolf."

"I remember."

Amy rubbed his arm. "Our alphas were so jealous of Hazel and River. They kept going on and on about how they deserved more in Tennessee."

"Why?" The chicken pot pie was amazing, I knew why it was Fern's favorite meal. I took bites whenever anyone else spoke.

"Well, they felt that they'd been forced to take the pack. Iris always wanted to take over in Florida, but they had an alpha. Everyone in Tennessee knew how much they wished they could switch. It left a sour taste in the pack runs."

Fern nodded. "Even the kids knew there was something off."

"Okay." I gave Fern a conspiratorial grin. "We recently figured out what factors go in to an epsilon wolf being born."

This got both Fern's parents attention. Amy's head tilted. "How did you figure it out?"

"A second and then a third epsilon on my doorstep." The shock rolled through the room. "To be fair, the third isn't a wolf yet." I reached over to clasp Fern's hand. "We won't get our third epsilon wolf until March."

There was a moment of silence, then Ronald's eyes widened. He was no idiot, and I watched in amazement as the secondary pigment of his aura shifted from blue to turquoise ... awe. "Pebble, alpha of the Wisconsin pack, I ... we, request to come and run with your pack in March."

Amusement filled me. When I shot a glance at Fern, I saw a smile on their face. Their secondary color had remained optimistic almost the whole time. "Yes, of course, I give you both permission."

My phone buzzed in my pocket. No one but pack knew this number. Checking the display, I saw it was Tanner. "I'm sorry, I have to take this."

I walked into the living room. Despite the distance, I was pretty sure the others could still hear the conversation, but I tried. "Pebble speaking."

"Check the news. There's been another death."

A boulder dropped into my belly. We'd only arrived ... we hadn't had enough time. "I assume you need us back tomorrow?"

"Yes. I believe they're trying to get our attention. I'm worried ... if they followed the two of you or know your itinerary, changing your plans is the only safe option."

Chapter 8 – On The Road Again

Another death.

I navigated on my phone to the story. There wasn't much information about the person, a young woman with light brown hair. The report said she was a college student who was in town visiting a friend.

In the kitchen, I sat, trying to pull my mind from the news Tanner had just dropped at my feet. I shook my head and faced Fern and their family. "There's been a development back home. I'm going to have to head back in the morning."

Fern winced. "So, we only have tonight?"

"I'm afraid so. I'm sorry this is being cut short." The weight of leadership felt like a boulder pressing down on me. "I mean, you *could* stay here—"

"No," Ronald said, an edge to his voice.

"I agree." My voice sounded strong, laced with a confidence I didn't feel. "Fern should come back with me. We're not sure what the end goal of this group is, though we've determined a few things."

For the next few minutes, I explained what we knew of Trista, the lone wolves that had escaped California and the Dynasty, and what we thought was going on. "Despite the fact that they're targeting Wisconsin, I think you're on the list as well. I don't think this group is big, and they probably won't be foolish enough to directly confront us at the pack den. That's the safest place right now."

Amy slid her arm around Fern's shoulder, her aura turning almost a full purple. *Darn it ... what does that mean? I really need to study more.* "As much as I want to keep my child close, I think you're right. Ronny and I are at work during the day and Fern would be here alone. They don't have a wolf yet." A small smile played across her face. "Yet."

I leaned back and gazed at the people around the table, deciding to ignore the colors. They were giving me a headache and frustrating me more than helping. "Have you two thought about returning to Tennessee? With Iris and Kendall gone, the pack needs alphas who understand what it means to lead and love the state where you live. You two could lift the Tennessee pack to where it should be."

Ronald's face tightened and despite my decision to ignore it, the red of rage was clear as day. "Again, like I told you on the phone, I don't want to go back there." He turned to Amy. "Do you?"

She sighed. "Part of me does. You know my family lives there. I do miss the area, but I'll support you and what you want. I don't like the idea of you miserable. I've found peace living here."

He grunted, and the flash of rage dimmed back to the blue of disapproval from when we'd first arrived. He finished off his meal. "Okay, I'll think about it. I like it here in Kentucky. I do miss having other wolves around, but I'm still not convinced leading is the right move for me and Amy ... not anymore."

After that, we switched the conversation to where epsilon wolves came from. As we spoke, Amy pulled out some bowls and dished up ice cream. Halfway through the bowl, Ronald smiled wide. "Well, it sounds like I'll have to return one of River's calls. He and I have to compare notes, see if the same wolf bit both of us. I'm glad that jerk was taken out, but at the same time, he seems to have been pretty powerful. Three alphas who then had three epsilon kids. Amazing."

His enthusiasm was infectious and the energy in the room lightened.

We spent the rest of the night talking about less important matters. Fern and I went to bed early so we could leave early the next day.

Two hours into the drive, Luna's mom called for my lesson. "Hi, Serena, I'm driving from Kentucky to Wisconsin right now, can we skip today? I'm not sure I can focus on both the lesson and traffic."

There was a moment when the line went silent, then she sighed. "You know these lessons are very important, right?"

"I do. But—"

"Can I call you back at eight this evening? I'm busy until then."

Part of me wanted to scream, but I had a feeling the only way to learn was to jump through her hoops. "Thank you for your understanding."

"Don't thank me yet, Pebble. Eight. And after that, nine in the morning. I've already rearranged my schedule for the next week for you. Please, no more last-minute changes."

"Okay, I promise." In the back of my mind I really hoped this was a promise I could keep.

As the hours droned on, we made it through Indiana, then Chicago. On the other side, we stopped for lunch. It was late, but we wanted to get the lion's share of the drive past us.

After we ate, Fern took over driving. "Do you have any music on your phone you'd want to listen to? This temp phone is empty."

Fern harrumphed as they continued to drive towards home. "You know, with our talk last night and us dropping into bed, then quickly dashing to the car, I never did charge my phone. And the charger is still safely packed in my bag. I honestly didn't think about it."

Amused, I watched the trees and homes pass by outside the car. "We could stop, and you could find your charger."

"No." They sighed. "It isn't worth it. We'll be back to the pack house soon enough. I can't think of anyone who'd call me anyway. Everyone knows we're together."

I shrugged. "That's true. People are probably just giving us our space."

Almost at the Madison exit, we made one more stop. We decided we needed ice cream ... or frozen custard. Culvers, a Wisconsin icon of a restaurant, called to me, so we went in and each ordered a waffle cone. I took over the driving, as we enjoyed the treat and finished the last leg of the tip home.

Fern gaped at the cone. "I can't believe how many good ice cream options there are in this state. Why aren't we having a different ice cream every night? Why did Dayna only set up a competition with pizza and cheese curds? All of you are so jaded with what's right in front of you."

"I mean, we could, if that's what you want. We'd have to set some rules, but I'm game." I waggled my brows. "First thing back at the pack den."

With a snort, Fern relaxed in their seat. "I'll have to talk with Dayna, have her add it to the website. Considering it's ice cream, though, she probably already has."

When we pulled up to the house, there weren't too many cars. I recognized several pack vehicles, including Tanner and Clare's. The only surprise in the driveway was Hollis's car. More surprising was Hollis herself climbing out, her face as tear-streaked as the last time I'd seen her.

Chapter 9 – A Misunderstanding

My heart sank in my chest when I saw Hollis. Her green base aura was swirling fast with blue and purple. I wanted to look at my notes but didn't want to sit here while she stood there crying. I knew grief was part of the blue, but I thought disgust was mixed in with the purple. Did I—or we—disgust her? What could be so wrong that she came here? Was it something with her? Someone in her family? Was Tanner wrong about who the lone wolves attacked? Was it someone Hollis knew? Was it someone we knew?

A quiver of fear ran through my body as I jumped from the car and ran to her. "What's wrong? Are you okay? Is anyone hurt?" My voice shook with worry as I asked the questions.

We embraced when I reached her, her sniffling echoed in the shaking of her body. Behind me, I heard Fern approach, their calming nature surrounding us both.

Finally, Hollis gulped in some air, her body still trembling. "Are *you* two okay? I've been trying to get ahold of you, but both your phones went right to voicemail. I thought ... but you're here, and together." She pulled back and punched my arm. "Why aren't you answering your phone?"

Not wanting to laugh at her gruff and sudden change of mood, I pulled her in for another squeeze, then stepped back. "My phone was stolen."

Her shoulders drooped. "Oh, I guess that makes sense." Then she focused over my shoulder. "But what about you?"

Fern stepped around me so we could all see each other. "We drove to speak with my parents. On the way down, my phone died."

Hollis swung again, swatting Fern's arm. "Why can't you keep your darn phone charged? Haven't we talked about this? The damn thing *can* be charged, you know. And for two days?"

From the corner of my eye, I saw Fern trying not to smile. "I promise to work on that ... I just ... I guess I didn't think you'd try to get ahold of me. Everyone else knew how to get a hold of Pebble by her temp phone. I'm sorry."

We all stood in the driveway for a minute staring at each other, breathing hard. Finally, I asked, "But, Hollis, why are you here?"

Her eyes widened. "Didn't you see the news? A college student, here visiting, staying in one of the suburbs of Madison, with sandy hair, was found dead in a park downtown. What was I supposed to think?"

The news article I'd read played through my mind. "I read that the person had light brown hair."

Hollis shook her head. "That was the first report. A second one came out, once the victim had been cleaned and the 'more information' came out. It sounded so much like Fern I started trying to get ahold of you, but then neither of you were answering your phones. At first I thought you may be busy, but then it continued." Her gaze drilled into me. "You *never* go that long without answering my texts. I *knew* there was something wrong."

Puffs of air blew from her mouth as Hollis's breathing got faster. She started to pace and rub her hands. "I decided that if I hadn't heard from you by dinner, I'd come over. But then I got here, and I didn't know what to do. I've never really been here, and your house is so damn big. I know your parents are in Tennessee, and what is *that* about?" She waved her hands. "I don't really want to know, I mean, I do, but not right now. At least, not if it's a lie."

There had never been a time I wished for epsilon calm more. I knew Conner was close, but there was no easy way to get him out here. I clasped Hollis's arms. "Hollis. It's really cold. Can we go inside? Maybe we can figure this all out. Fern and I have spent the better part of the last two days driving. I really don't know what's going on. But maybe we can all get answers in there. And as I said before ... no more lies."

At first Hollis shook her head, looking back and forth between me and the house. Finally, she sighed. "Yeah, okay. I am cold. But are there a lot of, um, wolves in there?"

I slid one arm around her. "Everyone in there is a person first. Don't worry. We can go directly to my room if you want. But getting coffee in the kitchen sounds really appealing."

Her head started shaking before I finished speaking. "Just your room, please."

The three of us headed in. There were people in the living room and kitchen. Conner and Estrella looked to be cooking. It smelled suspiciously like pasta and maybe garlic bread. Luna, Dayna, Tanner, and Clare were in the living room. Tanner stood when we got in.

I held up a hand. "We'll be just a minute. I need to talk with Hollis. Can whatever it is you need to say wait?"

A low growl came from him, but he nodded. "Yes. We do need to discuss what's going on, and I don't want to put it off. That said, Tyler said he'd be here at seven."

I checked my watch. "Okay, seven it is."

It wasn't until the door shut and Hollis sat at my desk that she visibly relaxed. "Am I safe here?"

Like at her house, Fern and I sat on the bed. "Of course you are. Why wouldn't you be?"

"Well, everyone here is a wa- ... wa- ..., um, wolf, right? Aren't wolves dangerous?"

Anger and frustration threatened to surface. Slowly, I breathed in and out, then gave Hollis a small smile, forcing myself to stay calm. She didn't know anything about this world, and at least she was asking questions. I felt Fern put a hand on my lower back, and the contact helped.

"Hollis, I understand that this is all new to you. I get that you're trying to figure a lot of things out, and I appreciate you're asking questions, but please understand I'm the same person you've been best friends with for years. You've never been unsafe with me before. Why do you think it's different now?"

She bit her lower lip and seemed to fold into herself. Then she released her held breath, dropping her head back to gaze up at the ceiling. Fern and I waited as Hollis sat there, her scent a swirl of nutty apprehension and woodsy determination. After one more sigh, she straightened and looked at me. "I don't know. When the word ..." Her voice lowered to a low whisper. "Werewolf." Her eyes darted back and forth as if a wolf would jump out of my closet or from under my bed. "It just brings up images of being attacked and forced to become one ... you know?"

Before she finished, I was shaking my head. "No, Hollis, I don't know. I was brought up in this house and it was the only place I ever felt safe. To me, this is where you go to get away from the monsters."

She froze, then said in a small voice, "Are there really monsters out there?"

"Can you ask that after you were attacked last weekend?" I scooted back until I could lean against the wall. "Look, in this house, we're pack wolves. We're like a big, mostly happy family. There are some other wolves that are ... I don't know, not as happy. But there are people everywhere that I would say are horrible ... in most cases, I'd call *them* the real monsters. That isn't something that is limited to werewolves."

I shot a glance at Fern then faced Hollis again. "Your instinct was right. That person ... that student—the one you thought could be Fern—we think they were attacked by a wolf. At least, I'm assuming that's what Tanner wants to talk to me about. We know *who* is behind the attack—"

"Good! So, call the police," Hollis cut in, her eyes wide.

Dread filling me, I rubbed my face. "It isn't that easy. Werewolves have to change into wolves once a month. They *can* change at other times. The police can't easily hold one of us. The first time we're given outside access, the culprit is gone. Not to mention, if someone is diabolical enough, they could start creating a pack of werewolves from the other inmates, and the guards wouldn't stand a chance."

My goal wasn't to scare my friend, but unfortunately, I knew from how quickly all the color drained from her face, I had succeeded in doing just that. Every word I said made the situation worse.

Fern leaned forward. "Most werewolves are good people. They have a family, they go to work, pay bills, and once a month, sing tribute to the moon. The biggest difference between a werewolf and a norm is a pack werewolf lives with others like them. Our family ... our *chosen* family is large, and loud, and boisterous, and caring. Everyone watches out for each other. We take care of each other. And in a situation like we're in now, we can all come together to protect each other. The stronger wolves protect the weaker ones."

"So, that big guy wants to protect you two?" Hollis waved in the direction of the living room.

"No." This was it. I thought someone had said something about this in the alley, but so much else had happened, maybe Hollis missed it. "I'm the alpha. I'm the strongest wolf in the pack. I protect everyone else. Tanner is strong, as is his son, and when we find this group, they'll be there. But in the end, I'll be there, too. I *will* protect my own."

Hollis's eyes widened, but she didn't say anything to me, she just turned to Fern. "What about you?"

Fern waved their hands. "I'm not a wolf, not yet at least. No fighting for me."

"Do you want to be a wolf?" There was skepticism and doubt in Hollis's tone.

"I do," Fern said, with a wide smile. "It's always been a dream of mine. It usually happens between the ages of seventeen and maybe twenty or twenty-one. I told my dad when I was young I wanted to be bitten if I wasn't a natural wolf."

There was a pause, then Hollis nodded. "Okay, thank you both for clearing that up. Werewolves aren't dangerous by nature. There are some ..." She paused, uncertain of the word.

"Lone wolves. Wolves without a pack."

"Fine. Lone wolves in town who are here because?"

We spent a few minutes explaining the bare basics of why Trista and her pals were around. I didn't want to get too in depth but gave Hollis enough so she knew what was going on.

"Got it. Okay." Her knuckles turned white from how tightly she clenched her fists. "I think I'll go home." For a moment she locked her jaw, then she shook her head and her hands out, as if realizing how tightly she held all her muscles. "Right now my head is spinning. There has been so much information, I don't know what to think. My heart wants to stay here and be with my friends, the two people I love more than anyone but my parents. But my head wants to run and hide, screaming all the way. Until I can find a happy medium, I ... I don't know."

We walked to the door in silence. A small flame of hope burned in the pit of my stomach, though I worried my hope came too soon. Hollis had come, but she was running just as quickly.

When Hollis got halfway to her car, she turned. "Goodbye, Pebble. Goodbye, Fern."

Fern's eyes closed and they looked like someone had punched them in the gut. As we watched Hollis drive away, they whispered, "Please come back."

Chapter 10 – Finding A Mole

Tyler showed up for dinner. I didn't know if he was happy to be part of my inner circle, but then again, I wasn't sure if he knew either. But, with electronics being part of the battle, we needed our expert.

We decided to wait until after we ate to discuss current events. At just after seven-thirty, we all headed up to the office: me, Tanner, Clare, Tyler, and Luna.

The first thing Tyler did was hand me my phone. "We found this at Trista's apartment."

Gazing down at the device, it looked lifeless. I pressed the button, but nothing changed. *I guess it needs to be charged, just like Fern's.* Despite everyone assuming Trista had my phone, the betrayal burned within me as I raised my focus to Tyler. "She had my phone for almost a week? Did she get in?"

He winced and with a force of effort, I tamped back any show of my power. After taking a shaky breath, he straightened his shoulders and said, "No. And since she tried to log in ten times, the safety lockout wipe was activated. You'll have to load from backup, or we can get you a new phone."

The update frustrated me, but I kept a blank face and merely nodded. "Okay, my phone is a bit old. It's been stolen once. I'd like a new one with all the safety features. Dad mentioned this before I headed to college, but I didn't see a reason. I think it's time." I shot a look at Luna. "How about you? With the extras, your phone would be protected. Either way, you should let Tyler add the pack protection package ... no extra cost either way."

The side of her mouth curved up. "Can I get one in pink?"

I shivered but Tyler merely nodded as his gaze turned to me. "With yours, I'll stick with blue. We should speak with the other new pack members. Make sure their phones are up to our standards."

"Sounds good." Tyler opened his phone and took some notes. "I'll have something here tomorrow for the two of you. We'll see about the others after the meeting."

"Thank you." I thought back on the rest of what I'd been told. As they replayed in my head, the important words hit me like a sack of bricks. "She has an apartment? Like her own? Or is she staying with a friend? One of the other wolves?"

"Oh no," Tanner's voice was low and full of anger. "She has her own place. From what I can gather, she's been in the same place since she got to Wisconsin."

I closed my eyes and had to take stock. "What did she do while she stayed here? We need to do a full sweep of the house, and an inventory ... if that's even possible."

Clare nodded. "Yeah. Estrella traced her finances. She has savings that go back to when she lived in California. Apparently, her parents set up an account and when they passed a few years ago, she and her brother both got a pretty big lump sum. She has no need to worry about money, not any time soon."

At her words, I held up my hands to get them to slow down. There were so many things I had to unpack. Everything I knew about this person was a lie. I guess I shouldn't have been surprised, but I had to give my brain a moment to process how very little I knew about someone taking up residence in my head.

With a shudder, I blew out air. "Okay, so she's rich *and* has a brother. I guess I should've guessed that, since she obviously knew about werewolves. Or did Quinn tell us that? Why do I feel like there's been a mountain of information over the last few days?" I took notes on a pad.

It was a way of settling my nerves. "Is the brother in town? Could it be one of the wolves we've already dispatched?"

"No," Tanner said, his face hard. "From everything we've learned, the brother lives in Oklahoma. He hasn't been part of any of this." His posture told a different story—he was wary.

Tyler nodded. "Apparently, he got a college degree and is working in a company there. We don't have a lot of information on him ... we don't have anyone down there we can tap to check in, but from everything we can tell digitally, he has a job, he's a worker of decent standing, and not a player on the board."

Luna grunted. "Can we keep an eye on him? I know we don't see him as an issue, but I still don't like having him as a non-issue. If it were my family, I'd be pissed."

Everyone in the room gazed at her. I worked to keep a blank face. I knew what Luna was like angry, and there was no denying she was scary.

Finally, Tyler gave a curt nod. "I can dedicate someone from Stone Security to keep an eye on the business he works for with a focus on him. I can explain that we're considering recruiting him. If I do that, I'll be informed of any change in his routine without our interest causing any red flags."

"What else did you find?" I still seethed at the idea of how well Trista had played me. With every fiber, I tried to keep my emotions under control. Luna placed her hand on my lower back, and I finally could take in a full breath.

Tanner leaned forward, elbows on his knees. "Easton did a full search of Trista's place. He used care to not leave evidence of his passing, thanks to the bear soap products. He took pictures of what he found, and he and I have been combing through everything. One of the big things we found was a notebook of the kills around town and who did them. It was both the tourists and the people from their group taken out by our pack. She was keeping track both ways."

Something in his voice had me pausing in my notes to look up at him. "Okay, what are you hinting at?"

"That kill, the one that happened last week? The one just off Willy Street?" Tanner's voice had taken a cold edge.

"I remember. Trista told me she'd been out that night with a friend from one of her classes. He'd really angered her, and she'd cut off all communication with him after that."

Tanner huffed out a laugh void of all humor. "Yeah, I'll say. The person she'd been with that night wouldn't ever talk with her again. She was the one who'd taken the kid out. But here's the thing, Pebble, we did a thorough search. She wasn't going to school. We checked her records in the apartment and there was nothing to indicate a student. That got us confirming with the college. It took some hacking," Tanner bowed his head to Tyler in acknowledgement. "But she's not a student at Madison College. Never has been."

The pencil I'd been writing with snapped in my hands. I snarled. "Sorry. I just hate that we couldn't smell or hear any of her lies. Moreover, I can't believe how well she fooled me. Gah! I'm such an idiot."

Luna chuckled. "She's a sociopath. She convinced herself of her story when she was with you so that she wasn't lying. It's the only way."

The anger and embarrassment dug deep, threatening to eat me from the inside. I could feel my body temperature rising with my fury. "What do we do next?" My voice was low, tight with my control.

"Easton put tiny trackers on most of her things. Once she gets home and moves anything from the apartment, we'll be able to follow her. It won't take long for us to corner her, question her, and end this." There was a finality to Tanner's voice. He'd been an ender his whole life.

"You aren't doing this alone," I said, with just as much conviction.

"No, I'll have Easton with me." His eyes bored into me, daring me to say more.

"And me. I'm the alpha, I'm *her* alpha, and I have power. I'm going to be there, too."

Tanner sat up tall. "Yes, you *are* the alpha, and we need you here, leading. You aren't expendable." The unspoken words that he was echoed in the room.

"If you think Trista and her cronies are a threat to me, you're wrong. You *will not* leave me behind. I'm going to be there when you end this."

Luna placed her hand on my arm. "Pebble, he's right. This group wants you to be there, they want me there as well. Their plan is to destroy the packs, I can feel it in my soul. Is this what your premonitions are like?" She shook her head and swallowed. "You can't be there." Her free hand lifted to her chest, and she rubbed. "Let Tanner and his son do their job. That's how packs work, right? Everyone relying on everyone else."

Clare smiled wide. "You know, I think I like this new alpha." She gave me a wink. "Why don't you sleep on it and we can talk about it more this weekend? For now, all we can do is wait."

I knew they all spoke reason, but despite that, I wanted to howl my frustration to the moon.

Chapter 11 – Changing The Rules

"Can we go for a walk?" After my workout and shower, I found Luna in the kitchen, or rather, she was there waiting for me.

"Now? Or can it wait until after my first mug of coffee? Maybe one of the muffins in that box over there." I wasn't sure who bought the muffins, but they made me pretty excited.

Luna sipped her own coffee. "Sure, it can wait a few minutes, but I was hoping we could talk outside of the house."

After pouring a cup of coffee and selecting an apple muffin, I sat and pulled out my temp phone. In the weather app, I checked, and it was a decently warm day ... for January in Wisconsin. Unlike earlier in the week, a walk would be doable.

We sat in silence as I drank my go-go juice and ate. Once I was done, we both cleared our dishes, got coats, and headed out.

Luna didn't know the area, so I led us to the bike trail. We walked south for about five minutes in blissful silence, enjoying the day ... at least I was.

"We didn't get off to a good start when we met."

With a bit of effort, I didn't laugh at her understatement. Thinking back on all our interactions from September through ... well, about two days ago when she agreed to help me lead, I could do nothing more than agree. "True. I'm not sure you like many people upon first meeting them."

She sighed. "You're not wrong. It's a goose thing. We are family-centric ... gaggle-focused. Once we decide who belongs to us, we are fiercely protective. We are violently apathetic towards anyone who isn't part of our group,."

"Is that, like, an instinct?" *Why do I feel she was more than apathetic towards me?*

"Yeah. When I was in high school I tried to fight it, but I had to choose between exploding and depression. In the end, I stayed with my crowd, it was easier for everyone."

"Were there many family members at your school? Was it like here with the pack? Lots of options to be with your extended gaggle?"

Luna started nodding before I finished speaking. "Exactly. I had a few of our people who went to the same school with me. We were our own group. A lot of people thought we were the 'mean girls,' but mostly we just ignored everyone else."

A runner passed, going in the same direction as us, while a biker zoomed by going in the opposite direction. Luna's nose twitched and she sneezed. My mouth curved up, but I tried not to show too much amusement. "We'll have to get you and Dayna out to the mall this week and to other places with people." I thought for a moment. "Probably Conner, too. The two of you have two animals and he's a new enough wolf that the scents and emotions of people are going to be intense. When we get back to college, especially in the dorms and in classes, it's going to be harder than you think."

First, Luna grunted, as if this weren't anything big, then she sneezed as a group of four bikers passed us. It looked like her eyes were watering. "Fine, you're right. You win."

This time, I did chuckle. We hadn't been debating, but it was nice to know I'd won the argument anyway. "So, learning about your background is interesting, but is that why you wanted to take this walk?"

"No. It's ... well, it's complicated. You may have noticed that last week I started being nicer around you."

My mind stuttered to a screeching halt at this. Only years of dealing with outlandish statements from my brother Owen kept me from blurting out something that may have been considered argumentative. Instead, I just waggled my hand back and forth in a 'sort of' gesture.

Luna's eyes narrowed. "Okay, well, it's true. Once I got my wolf, I started feeling the pull of being an alpha. It scared me, and I knew you were the cause of all the changes. I may have lashed out once or twice, but I also *didn't* lash out a lot. I was friendly."

We walked for a few more steps while I processed what she considered 'nice.' Once I decided I had my voice under control I said, "Okay, I can think of times when we got along in the past week. I can see what you're implying. I'm still uncertain about the walk and why you wanted privacy."

"Well, I'm getting there." Her face scrunched up, and a cold breeze lashed at our bodies. Each of us tucked our hands into our pockets, trying not to get too cold. Finally, Luna sighed. "After the full moon run, something clicked in me. I don't know if it was my connecting with the wolf or truly accepting my place in the pack, but something shifted. I became more than a goose in wolf's clothing. I became pack."

The words warmed something deep within me and I reached out to take her hand. At first Luna hesitated, but then she pulled her hand from her pocket to take mine.

There was another stiff breeze, and we turned back towards home, still holding hands.

The trees swayed and, in the distance, there was the rustle of animals dashing in the underbrush. Luna continued. "More than feeling like I was truly an alpha ... I felt, no, I feel like I'm your partner. I don't know how to explain it, but I know that if we face this together, we can do anything." Her shoulders rose and she ducked her head a bit. The image so un-Luna like. "Does that sound silly?"

"No, not at all." I bumped her shoulder. "I think it's empowering. From the time I met you, I knew you were one of the strongest people I knew. If I have you in my corner, well, then, we can continue the legacy of this pack. I know it."

There was almost a purr from my wolf, something I only experienced when she was really happy. I didn't think Luna and I were out of the woods yet, but we were heading in the right direction for becoming strong pack leaders.

On the walk home, I received a text from Hollis asking if we could go to brunch the next day. She hoped that Fern and I could help answer some questions she had.

I texted back yes.

Once back to pack house, Luna and I gathered Dayna and Conner to head to the mall. We knew it wouldn't be as busy as around a holiday, but there'd still be people milling about, shopping, and trying to find a place to walk around away from the bitter cold wind. Fern wanted to come, so we all decided to go shopping.

The parking lot was emptier than I'd hoped. We ended up finding a spot close to a set of doors and scurrying inside. "This is just like walking around State Street." Dayna wrapped an arm around my shoulders. "Are you sure this will be all that bad? You know, maybe you're just worrying too much."

I gave a small shrug with my free shoulder. "We can always hope. Then you all can laugh at me. We'll get some cinnamon rolls and call it a day."

We entered through the main door instead of the food court. I figured the best plan would be building up to where the crowds were.

As we moved further into the mall, Dayna was the first to falter. "Oh. Gods." She paled. "There aren't even that many people, but ... oh. This is unpleasant."

Shops lined both sides of the wide hall, and in the center were small kiosks that sold shirts, cell phone accessories, and jewelry. There were proprietors running the stands, consumers shopping at the stores, and others milling about, gazing at everything. Kids ran around with sticky colored goo on their fingers, faces, and clothes. There was enough room to navigate, but the place wasn't barren.

Conner nodded slowly. "I'm glad it isn't just me." He rubbed his face. "There are so many ... and ... gods."

"You need to use all the words if you want us to know what you mean." Fern put a hand on his shoulder, and Conner took in a shaky breath.

"Oh." His gaze bounced around from the hoards of the tiny crowd in the mall to Fern. "Did you know wolves can smell emotions? And, like, hear everything. There is—" He slapped his hands over his ears and shook his head.

In the center of the large hallway, between a stand with snow globes and a second one selling kids' playing cards, were a bank of couches. It was back about a dozen feet away from most of the individuals. I slid my arm around Conner's waist and led him in that direction. I could feel the others follow.

Once everyone sat, I considered them. "This is what I've been trying to tell you. There are different ways of thinking about what's going on, boxes to shove everything you don't want to deal with, headspaces, or imagine yourself a queen or king of your own castle and build a wall around yourself to protect your inner you from all of that." I waved my hand, palm out, towards the mass of a dozen or so people.

The others all shut their eyes and got quiet. As they focused on controlling how they reacted to scents and emotions, I focused on the light show of auras around me. On my phone, I pulled up the notes ap and tried to summarize what I saw on different people and what it could mean. I knew I could take this to my next lesson with Serena.

A couple with their three kids came down the hall in our direction. The woman glowed green, social, nurturing. The man's hue was dominated with orange, thoughtful and considerate. Two of the kids shone a confident yellow, a friendly and charismatic color. The last was more empathic with an indigo. I wondered if that was the middle child.

As they passed, the youngest cried out for an ice cream. The others all flinched at the high-pitched sound.

Swiveling to look behind me, I saw the ice cream shop with all its enticing colors beckoning passersby. The mom stopped near us to calm her daughter, who kept emoting her frustration at not getting the sugary treat, and not getting it now! Her small, booted foot stamped; she wanted it right away.

Once they'd left, I walked each of the new wolves with me through some mental exercises, then, once they seemed to relax, we got ice cream and left. We'd return on Monday and maybe even Wednesday and Friday. Hopefully we'd make it to the food court and the scrumptious cinnamon rolls one of those days.

School started the following week, and we needed everyone up to being able to go to classes ... fast.

Chapter 12 – The Route To Friendship Is Through The Stomach

Luna woke up early and joined me in the gym. Like many of my family, I liked getting in and out of the gym when it was empty, but having Luna there seemed natural.

We didn't talk, we just moved through our routines in companionable silence.

After we finished, we each went to separate floors to shower and dress and met up in the kitchen for breakfast. "That was a good workout." She sipped her coffee. "You do that every morning?"

"Yeah."

"What about sleep?"

I laughed. "I don't do it as regularly during the school year. Classes are hard. But, yeah, during non-school days I usually get up early and start my day like this."

"What time is your first class?"

My cheeks heated. "Not until ten ... well, nine fifty-five, but yeah, ten."

Coffee almost came out of Luna's nose, which set me off. "You get up at ridiculous times, like, you're showered and dressed before the sun has even had her coffee, and you're skipping out on this because of a ten o'clock class? Are you kidding me?"

"You sound like my brother ... and dad. They both pushed me to join track or volleyball."

"Hmm." Luna got up and put a bagel in the toaster. "Do you want one?"

"No, I'm going to brunch with Fern and Hollis."

"When?"

"We're meeting Hollis at the diner at eleven."

Luna snorted. "You're going to not eat for the next four hours? How about a bagel?"

Her amusement hit home, and I smirked at my own ridiculousness. "Sure, sounds great."

"So, track, volleyball. I take it you were a real joiner in high school." There was a bit of a mocking tone to her statement, but nothing mean. *This is so much different.*

"Track is a bit of a family tradition. I also like the challenge of being good, but not too good to cause suspicion. But I really love the community of volleyball."

"Then why don't you join a team?"

So many people had asked me that. With a sigh, I sipped my coffee, letting it warm me as I thought about my reasons. "I guess part of me wanted to just blend in when I got to college. I know that sounds silly, there are thousands of students, the idea of standing out is not feasible. But joining a sport would mean more people would know who I was. I also knew I would eventually need to focus on alpha training. It would be my last free days to hang out with Hollis."

"You know, very little about you blends in. You may not be known on a global scale, but in both classes I was in with you, everyone knew who you were, and the professors loved you. As for the training, that ship has sailed. I think, if you want to run, or bat a ball, you should go for it."

"Bat a ball?" I bit my lip to stop from laughing.

"Whatever. I don't really know anything about sports. Do you want butter, jelly, fish, what? What do you want on your bagel?"

"Cream cheese and jelly."

"Gross, but whatever." She shook her head then searched the refrigerator for what each of us wanted.

"Have you ever had it, or are you just being really judgmental?" One of my eyebrows rose in challenge.

"I'll try yours, then do cream cheese and lox on mine. We finally got the proper ingredients in this behemoth of a house."

Luna prepared mine and tasted it. Her face scrunched up and she shrugged. "It isn't wholly awful ... I guess. Maybe a dessert bagel, if there were no better dessert options." She placed the plate in front of me and went to finish preparing hers.

"Why don't you join track? We could sign up together? You could learn the love of being part of something bigger than yourself."

She looked at me over her shoulder, her face hard. "You mean like joining a werewolf pack to help lead?"

A laugh bubbled out of me as we sat and enjoyed our post exercise breakfast.

When we were done, she narrowed her eyes on me. "You know, if we're going to lead together, we really should know more about each other."

My stomach clenched, and I began to regret eating. Part of me hoped someone else would join us soon. It wasn't that I didn't want to know more about Luna, it was just that the way she looked at me ... it was slightly terrifying. "Um, okay. Did you have something specific in mind?"

A smile slowly spread across her face and for some reason a scene from the cartoon, *How the Grinch Stole Christmas*, flitted through my mind. "Yes. Follow me."

She led me back to the barn. "I debated doing this outside, but it's too cold today. There's enough room here, so this will work."

"Work for what, Luna? You still haven't told me what we're doing." I could hear the edge in my voice.

"You haven't really seen my goose."

It took me a second, then I forced my mouth to shut, and I closed my eyes, reopening them less wide. "What? Now?"

Luna chuckled softly, and I could almost feel it in my soul. "Scared, alpha?"

I licked my lips. "No, it's just ... I mean, no. I'd love to see your goose." My words got a bit breathy by the end. I knew Luna could tell I was nervous.

Leaning over, she kissed my cheek. My heart beat faster and my hands trembled. "Don't worry, it'll just be me. And I'm not scary at all."

Without being able to stop it, I snorted, then slapped my hands over my mouth. Luna winked, took a couple of steps back, then squatted down.

It was totally unfair in my opinion that shifter birds could keep their clothes on when they found their animals. A dark gray, almost black, fog encompassed Luna, and a moment later a goose stood in the middle of the gym.

Her body was mostly black, though white peeked out. Her neck and the top of her head were black, with a white stripe that went under her chin.

I took a slow breath, then squatted down and reached out to touch the top of her head. Right before I made contact, Luna honked. Startled, I tensed, toppled back on my butt, then rolled until I lay fully on my back. My arm flopped over my eyes, and I stayed like that until my heart rate slowed.

Once I felt calm, I sat up, cross-legged. Luna's head bobbed, as if she was laughing. The image of me startled and falling back, terror on my face, flashed in my mind. My shoulders slumped. "Really? You're sending me *that*?"

She came over and ducked her head under my hand. I froze but finally stroked down her neck and over her back feathers. She was a lot softer than I expected. After a few minutes, I finally relaxed and she pecked at my cheek, much as she'd done before shifting.

After that, she backed away and the dark cloud covered her body again. In a very short amount of time, the person was back.

Luna grunted. "It's hard shifting so quickly and not flying." She shook her head. "And I'm so much heavier with these bones. It's nice being a bird once in a while."

"Yeah, Jade said when she was pregnant, her swan form was amazing to alleviate the stress from all the extra weight and discomfort of carrying kids."

"That makes sense." Luna sat across from me. "I still can't believe she wouldn't fly with me."

I laughed. "There are videos of her as a swan being attacked by geese. I think she fears what would be uploaded to the California pack's website if you two flew in harmony. 'Jade's finally lost it and switched teams ... bird teams that is.'"

Luna smiled. "You and your family are all odd, you know that?"

I waggled my brows. "You're one of us now."

Hollis wanted Fern and me to meet her at a diner near campus. I knew that the spot was popular, even when classes weren't in session, so we arrived early to get a table. The wait wasn't as long as we'd thought it would be, but I was glad we'd got there when we did.

Tyler had stopped by pack den before we'd left, so I had my new phone. He'd even got my original number transferred over. Downloading my backup had taken time, but I now had a phone that felt familiar.

Once we were seated, I sent Hollis a text, letting her know I had my original number back, and where she could find us in the restaurant.

She texted back she'd be there in five minutes and to order her coffee.

Fern rubbed my arm. "Just breathe. It's going to be fine. You know she wouldn't ask for this to tell us she'd decided she was done with us. It's going to be okay."

Though my brain told me Fern was right, my heart kept lying to my soul. I couldn't help but worry. "I know, I just ... okay, everything will be fine, you're right."

The five minutes slipped by, and Hollis was shown to our booth by one of the wait staff. She immediately sipped her coffee. I'd already doctored it the way I knew she liked it. She sighed. "Thank you! It's just what I needed."

The server came over and we ordered our food. Then it was time to relax and wait. The diner was full, so we knew it wouldn't be quick.

Hollis sipped more coffee. "What is it about diner coffee? It's always a bit burnt tasting, but also, it always tastes ..."

I laughed. "Like friendship? Like late night laughing and gossiping, not wanting to go home on a school night?"

"Exactly!" Her smile lit her face as I described any number of evenings from our shared past. Her shoulders drooped. "But are my memories all fake?"

My body tensed. I didn't want to dismiss her worries. Wanting to reassure her, I slowly reached across the table to clasp her hands in mine. "No, nothing was fake. Our time together, our friendship, our jokes and history, Hollis, it's all real. I just had one small thing I couldn't tell you ... or anyone really. But you know about it now. Ask me anything, I'm literally an open book."

"If I asked would you ... you know." She pulled a hand from one of mine and waved it between me and Fern.

I searched her face. Her jaw was clenched, and her eyes were wide with fear. "Yes and no. It isn't something done on a whim. That said, if we spoke and you went through some training, and you really wanted to join the fray, then yeah, it would be something that is on the table. But you don't need to do that to be part of our group. There are friends who are in the know that join us each month. They don't run, but they're there for the rest of it. Partners of ... you know."

We were all trying to avoid using the word wolf or werewolf. Being in a public place made this more complicated, but I thought it made Hollis more comfortable.

A server brought our food, so I leaned back, opening up more table space for plates. "Do you need a refill?"

"Yes, please. All of us," Fern answered before any of the rest of us could.

"Do you need anything else right away?"

Everyone shook their heads.

The food was amazing and for the next minute or two we all just ate. Then Hollis asked, "Okay, I really need to understand about Luna. Like, I don't get it."

My breath hitched as the enormity of the question hit me, quickly followed by amusement. I barely understood Luna, much less how to explain her. But I had told Hollis to ask anything. "To understand that, I'll need to start at the beginning, which is a really long story."

"Are we in a hurry?" Hollis took a bite of her chocolate chip waffle.

The enormity of what I was about to do slammed into me. "No, but ... okay. Let me tell you all the things I've never told you before." I rubbed my face. "This is going to be a lot, my friend. I hope you're ready."

Eyes wide, Hollis nodded.

For the next hour I told Hollis about my birth parents, their deaths, my adoption, and how being a wolf from such a young age was not normal or safe. Fern added their thoughts on wolf lore and what being bitten so young meant. Then I went on to tell my friends about the premonitions and the training my dad had been working on with me for years.

"So, you had a premonition about Luna?"

My body felt drained. "Yeah, you know that nightmare I'd been having?"

Hollis's jaw dropped open. "That was a premonition?"

"Yeah, it was telling me about someone I needed to find to help me lead."

"And that someone is Luna? For real?"

A laugh bubbled out of me. "Yeah, it took a while to figure that one out, but by winter breaks class trip, I finally learned what all the pieces meant."

She sipped her coffee. "What if you're still interpreting it wrong? I mean, this is a big assumption, Pebble."

Fern reached over and rubbed Hollis's arm. "No, there are too many indications that this is correct."

"But will Luna run your group into the ground, or just leave? Is she really the right choice?"

As much as I wanted to scream, I owed my friend the answers she wanted. "In the end, I believe Luna could be excellent." For a moment, the truth behind my words even shocked me.

"Has living with Luna been as fun as it sounds?"

I couldn't help the smile that split my face which quickly morphed into a laugh. It felt so cathartic. "It's getting better. She *is* nice to people she feels are 'her' people. I think I'm slowly getting to be in that category."

The subject needed to be changed, so I leaned forward and waggled my eyebrows. "There was a second premonition about an additional member joining the group. Ironically, there was nothing about Fern."

Hollis gaped, then narrowed her eyes. "Dayna?"

That lessened the tension, and we all finished our meals, talking about the weeks following my understanding of the premonitions.

Once the server returned for the final time asking, "Do you need anything else?", I knew I was ready for the big question. Reaching over, I clasped Hollis's hands in mine. "Where does that leave us?"

Hollis smiled. "I want to go back to where we were, I really do. I'm trying. I just need my mind to catch up with my soul. This last week has been horrible. I miss my friends, my people. The thought of college without the two of you sounds dull and depressing. It may take me time to really fully adjust to all this new information, but I think I'll get there."

Fern smiled. "Does that mean you want Pebble to stay your roommate?"

Hollis snorted. "Yeah, it does. I mean, she's the one with the coffee maker." I couldn't stop the laugh as I thought about the coffee the dorms served. The others were laughing, too. She continued, "I can't fathom not having that. And, Pebble, you signed up for Spanish this semester. You'll fail without my help."

I scoffed. "You're not wrong there."

A somberness came over Fern. "Do you think you'd ever want to ... you know, become like Pebble?" Though Hollis knew Fern would one day be a werewolf, she still didn't know Fern would wolf out in March. That was a discussion for another day.

"I don't know." A far off look came over Hollis face. "But right now my answer is no."

Chapter 13 – Back To The Real World

Sunday night, I sat in the living room reading a book. Part of me couldn't believe I'd finally achieved the ultimate winter break activity. There was one week left before school started and I planned on doing as little as possible.

Cuddled under a blanket, enjoying a mug of hot chocolate, I finally let myself get lost in the story, momentarily forgetting the world around me ... if that was even possible.

My phone rang and I snarled low, glaring at the noise. If it weren't new, I may have tossed it against a wall. Across the room, Fern laughed. "I don't think you'll scare the thing. That new contraption Tyler got you is top of the line. It won't be afraid of the likes of you."

I tried not to laugh as I answered. "Pebble Stone, how can I help you?"

"Hi, Pebble, it's Kaitlyn." Her chipper voice, with its Minnesotan accent, cut across the line and for a moment I thought I could hear her blinking. *Can anyone be that excited and bubbly?* "I know when you asked for a month off from work, you hoped for all of winter break, but we really need to put you on schedule this week. Breaks are our busy time, don't you know. And you live in town right? I have the correct paperwork, don't I?"

I pinched the bridge of my nose, trying to sort through everything she'd said. This had to be about my job as a tour guide for the university. I could feel the stress inching its way up my shoulders towards my neck. When I'd applied, the application had been online. There was no 'paperwork' to mess up. "When I did what, now? What did I request?" Her chipper voice beat into my head like a ball-peen hammer, but for the life of me, I couldn't remember requesting so much time off.

"Before finals ... you know, you called and said you needed time off." Even though she didn't say 'duh,' I could hear it all the same.

I tried to speak slowly so Kaitlyn would understand. I feared she'd get lost in the details if I spoke at normal

Midwest speed. "Kaitlyn, I called before finals to tell you I was going on a one *week* school sponsored research project. I requested to be relieved from tours until the first of the year."

"Oh, my God!" she squealed. I had to hold the phone away from my ear. Even Dayna and Luna flinched across the room. "I am so silly." The girl sounded a few cards short of a full deck. "When I wrote down your request I wrote an 'M' instead of a 'W.' I do that all the time. It's so easy to do, right?"

Dayna covered her mouth with her hands, and I could feel Luna's disgust.

I shut my eyes tight, trying to think of a single instance where I would mess those two letters up. "I guess."

Luna rolled her eyes and shook her head. She could probably hear the lie.

"So that means you're available, right?"

For so many reasons, I wanted to say 'no.' For the first time since ... maybe before school started in August, I had downtime, and she was threatening to take it away. But I had made a commitment, and I wasn't about to back out. "Um, yes, it does." There was an edge of sad resignation to my voice.

"Oh, perfect. I'll put you down for two tours on Monday, Wednesday, and Saturday. This will be really helpful. So many people want to see the campus or have family visiting and just want to show off."

"I'm happy to help." I hoped she didn't hear the flatness in my voice.

Once I got off the phone, there was a chorus of giggles and laughs from around the house. I had the time to do the job, and bringing joy to my pack was a good thing ... right?

Monday, I got to Union South where the tour began. I arrived early, had my clipboard, and was ready as soon as my clients started to trickle in. The normalcy of the morning shocked my system, and I had to stop myself from laughing with glee at the freedom of being a regular college student for a couple of hours.

As much as I had grumbled at the idea of returning to work, now that I was here, my soul settled from the cool air, the people asking mundane questions, and being back on campus.

For a few hours, I don't have to worry about wolves, pack, or being alpha. It felt like I stood a few inches taller as all the weight of responsibility tumbled away.

The only thing that I didn't like were all the shiny auras. I'd finally gotten used to seeing them on my pack mates, they started to blend in, but now I had to adjust to figuring out why each person had the hues shimmering around them and if I needed to be concerned.

I could almost hear Serena from our lessons. *Pebble, this is a blessing, one that Luna never believed could be hers. Each tint represents a piece of the soul of the person you're looking at. It gives you an insight as to who they are. If you're willing to study the intricacies of the colors, how they relate to each other, and the personalities of people, you can evaluate the nuances and often know motivations before the people themselves know what they're going to do. Its power, werewolf alpha. Why wouldn't you want to embrace your newfound knowledge and master it? Dig deep and let the auras tell you a story.*

A couple with their son had checked in somewhere near the middle of the group of tourists. The older man had an orange aura, thoughtful and considerate. Swirling within his orange was a combination of light and dark green and a pinch of blue. The two tones of green were interesting, submission. The addition of blue brought in a bit of amazement or awe. Probably his excitement for the tour.

The woman had a red aura, energetic and strong-willed. A darker red and orange swirled quickly throughout her base tint. Aggression ... and a high amount of it. During the tour she pushed her husband to ask questions on the family's behalf.

When I looked closer, I could see he also had an underlying black tucked in within his orange. His base aura was starting to shift. He was being drained, becoming tired. Maybe he was pushed around too much. She had some brown clinging deep against her body, part of the aura tint. Her selfishness and insecurity were taking over maybe, or maybe they were disappearing.

I wish I could take a picture and send it to Serena and ask for her help.

The couple's son had a purple aura. He was empathic, which was probably hard with the emotions his parents gave off. Like his dad, he had turquoise swirling within the purple. He was in awe of what he saw. If I were to guess, he would be coming to UW-Madison after he graduated high school.

As I gazed at the other people in the group, I quickly assessed their auras, jotting down notes on the back of my list to discuss with Luna's mom during our meeting later.

At the start of the tour, I was a bit rusty. I hadn't been on campus in over a month, nor had I spoken to anyone but pack in that time. It took me about five minutes to find my groove and maybe another ten to stop focusing on the fact that all the people around me glowed.

Once the first tour was completed, I headed down to State Street for a burger and cheese curds. I knew I could stay by the Union, but I wanted to avoid my clients finding me and asking more questions.

Walking back to start the second tour, I realized I'd spent a lot of the previous few weeks sitting around the house. *Maybe getting back to work is even better. The longer I walk around, let the soul of the university seep in, the more connected to campus I feel.*

About a quarter hour before the second tour, the clientele started to show up. A mother and daughter who checked in first were wolves, but two other families squeezed in before I could figure anything out.

When I looked at my list for the second tour, I laughed to myself when I saw Conner's name. He arrived shortly thereafter. He waited for everyone else to get their name tags before checking in and getting his.

He leaned in close and spoke low. "Did you notice that the brunette with curly hair and her mom are wolves?"

With a curt nod, I smiled warily. Pride filled me that he'd noticed so quickly.

My pre-tour time ended and I turned to the group. "Okay, everyone, make sure your name tags are secured to your coats. I'm Penelope and I'll be your guide."

As I showed the group around campus, Conner was as interested as everyone else. It occurred to me we gave him a driving tour but never showed him more than State Street by foot. At least, I hadn't. Dayna could have, but she wasn't native to the area either.

About a third of the way into my speech, I mentally connected to Conner. His eyes widened. *'Pebble? Is that you?'*

One of the tour clients asked me a question. I quickly answered them and told them the direction we'd be heading next.

'Yes, it's me, I need you to text Tanner about the two wolves.'

'Oh, okay. I forgot that we could easily do this and keep our conversation private. Sorry.'

'No worries. Let's keep this open, then you can tell me what Tanner says ... unless you're getting a headache.'

There was a pause where I could almost feel his breathing slowly. *'No, I'm fine.'*

I continued to explain about the campus buildings and dorms, waving my arms in the appropriate directions. *'Have you had enough to eat? Did you bring a protein bar with you? You know I'm not carrying you anywhere.'*

A soft laugh echoed in my mind. *'Yes, Jade warned me to always carry food. I'll eat some in a minute.'*

We got to the next stop, and I explained the different buildings, what classes would be offered in each—generally—and the closest dorms. We were getting close to Library Mall.

'Okay, he knows. He'll be here soon.'

He dropped the connection and started to eat. I continued the tour. Knowing that Tanner would be there as backup settled my nerves. Not that this pair scared me, I just liked having backup. That's what pack was there for.

When we got to the end of the tour, everyone came to say a final word to me. Conner stayed nearby. The last client to approach me were the werewolf girl and her mom.

"Hi, Julep." She still wore her name tag.

Her eyes widened. "Is reading minds one of your abilities?"

"One of my tour guide abilities? Because, besides having a clipboard of knowledge, you're wearing the nametag of forget-me-not."

The girl blushed, slapping her hands to cover her face. For some reason, I didn't think she was one of the lone wolves we were looking for.

Her shoulders rose as if she wanted them to hide her face. "I'm so sorry, it's just ... Heather, she said to find you on a tour and showed me your picture. You're Pebble, right? Jade's sister."

In the distance, I saw Tanner step out from the shadows, his face an image of confusion. I was pretty sure it mirrored mine.

"Heather? Jade?"

The girl's mother stepped forward. "I'm sorry. Julep seems to have skipped a few steps. We're from Colorado. She's currently in Colorado about an hour from the pack. She wants to transfer here. She wanted to meet you and see the campus before she made a decision. Heather said you were really nice, and Julep would love you."

Tanner waved, turned on his heel, and walked away.

Conner stepped up to stand next to me.

The two from Colorado didn't notice Tanner, but they did see Conner. "Oh!" Tabatha, the mother, said. She also still wore a nametag. "We should go somewhere more private."

"Julep, Tabatha, this is Conner. He's one of mine." I smiled at Julep. "And like you, he's a transfer. He's from Florida and this will be his first semester here." Before they could say anything else, I continued. "Where are you staying? Why didn't you check in right away or better yet, call before flying here?" This practice was becoming epidemic. I'd need to bring it up at the next alpha meeting.

Tabatha's eyes widened. "Oh, I don't know why we didn't think to call. I guess that would've made sense. I just figured we'd see you here and it didn't matter."

"It always matters," I interrupted her.

She blushed, very much like her daughter. "And we have a flight heading back to Colorado leaving at eight tonight."

Conner's brow furrowed. "That's a short trip."

Eyes wide, Julep nodded fast. "I know. I really like the idea of transferring, but I have a friend's wedding coming up this weekend and she has a bunch of activities this week. She knew I was available and asked me to do most of the work. When I saw Pebble's name on the tour guide list," she shrugged, "we made a last-minute decision. And after we called Heather, I guess we just jumped on the next plane."

It took an effort to stop the growl from bubbling up from my gut. Standard werewolf procedure shouldn't be ignored. I forced a smile. "It's too bad you won't see more of the area or come see pack house. Remember, when you come again, call first, stay for a few days, really get the feel for our great city. We'd be happy to host you."

Both mother's and daughter's jaws dropped open. Then Julep smiled shyly. "Thank you, Pebble."

Chapter 14 – Mind Over Matter

Dayna decided to take Conner and Fern to the barn and work with them on potential exercise routines. It had taken me a few minutes to get my blanket cocoon exactly how I wanted it. I still had a few days to enjoy reading and relaxing before winter break ended. There hadn't been any news on Trista, there weren't any pressing things to teach the others about being a werewolf ... not today, and I wanted to read.

Next to me, someone sat, rocking the couch for a moment. I held up my right hand, my pointer finger slightly higher than the rest. *I will get to the end of this chapter if nothing else.*

Though having someone next to me distracted me, the story still grasped me in brilliance, and I read on. When I finished the chapter, I slipped a bookmark in, placed the book on the side table, and smiled over at ... Luna.

I should've known, there really weren't many others it could've been.

"Pebble, I want to talk. I don't think we should do it in front of the others, and I'm tired of the office ... and as nice as it is, I'm ready to be out of this house."

One of my brows rose. "Okay, what are you thinking?"

"We go to dinner tonight."

The side of my mouth quirked up in a half-smile. "Why, Luna, are you asking me out on a date?" Though I teased, my heart beat a bit faster. *Does she want to stay to help with the pack? Does she want to stay with me? Is this what Hollis always feels with other girls? Is my head going to explode?*

She rolled her eyes. For once it amused me, and my smile grew. Voice flat and one brow raised, she asked, "Is that a yes or a no?"

"Sure. Where do you want to go ... or, maybe I should ask what type of food? You don't know this area as well as I do."

"I wish there was edible seafood. I miss the good stuff." She sighed. "And I don't want a chain restaurant. I want something decent." She rubbed her eyes. "Do you know how delicious the food is out in Maine? Maybe we can go out there this summer ... or at some point, and you can taste what you're missing."

As she spoke, I'd started a search on my phone. I was pretty sure there were places in town that had decent options. I wasn't sure if they'd be up to her standards. "Do you want lobster, fish and chips, just a fish filet?" I continued to scroll. "There's a place that has really good clam chowder."

"White or red broth?" Luna snapped out quickly.

"New England, um, white."

"I *know* what New England clam chowder is, Pebble," she scoffed. "Remember? I'm the one who asked for this."

"Is this how all our dates are going to go?" I mumbled under my breath, ready for a nap.

She leaned over and kissed my cheek. "Probably, now let me go get pretty. Meet back here in an hour." Standing, she sauntered off.

My hand slowly lifted to where she'd kissed me. It wasn't the first time she'd done it, but before I thought it had been more ... ironic. *What is going on?*

Then her words caught up to me. *She's getting dressed up? Do I have to get dressed up?*

Untangling myself from the blanket, I sent a text to Brooke, outlining our conversation. I knew she'd be working, but hoped she'd be able to explain whatever it was that had just happened.

How was Owen so good at dating and you and Jade so bad? I'd made it to my room and started leafing through my outfits. *If you have any dresses, send me pictures. Then, next time you have a chance, go shopping, maybe with Hollis, I'm sure she's better at this than you are.*

I wasn't sure that was true. Maybe Julez? Did I have anyone who could help me? When I was younger I knew what worked with Jade. But over the years I had hidden with the pack. Dating had become anathema for me. Just because I knew what others should do didn't mean I understood how to interact with Luna.

Standing in the center of my room, I realized I was spiraling. I closed my eyes and took a deep breath. The different outfits I'd bought over the years flitted through my mind, and I realized I really didn't need Brooke, I had this. In a drawer of my dresser I found a navy blue skirt that stopped just above my knees. After searching, I found a pair of matching tights. In my closet, near the back, I selected a long sleeved, off-white, V-neck, fitted sweater.

After my shower, I was once again glad for my short hair that was easy to dry and style. I dressed, took a picture, and sent it to Brooke.

Looks good but add the necklace I gave you two Christmases ago, with the matching earrings.

Once done, I decided I looked as good as I got. I shook my head in amusement. *I can't believe I'm about to go on a date with Luna Zweck.*

The scent of hot chocolate wafted down the hall as I headed towards the living room. Fern, Conner, and Dayna sat in the kitchen, talking and laughing. As I approached, they all turned and smiled.

One of Fern's eyebrows rose. "Looking good, fearless leader. Is there a reason you're so ..." their hand waved back and forth.

While I was deciding how to respond, Luna's arm draped over my shoulder. I hadn't even heard her approach over their chatter and the draw of their drinks. "We're going out to dinner together. No, none of you are invited, it's an alpha thing. Now, be good pups and don't get into any trouble while mommy and mommy are out."

The slight widening of Fern's eyes at Luna's 'mommy and mommy' mirrored my internal reaction. I didn't know a person could be gobsmacked so many times in so few minutes, but apparently it was a thing. *Is this what dating is? A series of confused moments strung together in which a person doesn't know which way was up? Did Luna feel this way too, or was she the ringleader of my circus of unfettered emotions?*

Before any of us could respond, her hand slid down my arm to mine and she pulled me away from our friends. Before I could pull my coat from its hook on the wall, Luna pulled it down, and held it open for me to slip on. At my slightly baffled look, she smirked, waiting for me to slide my arms in. Once done, we headed out to one of the smaller cars.

Halfway to the restaurant, Luna smiled wide. "I didn't know you cleaned up so nicely, Pebble. If I had—"

With a smirk, I shot her a glance. "What, you would've asked me out sooner? Been nicer?" I chuckled. "I can't see anything happening any differently."

She barked out a laugh. "No, nothing like that. I wouldn't have worried about you embarrassing me tonight. I kept trying to figure out which snarky shirt you were going to pick out as your 'fancy' shirt."

A sense of lightness filled me as we made our way across town to the restaurant.

Being a Monday night, it didn't take long to be seated. We spent a few minutes looking over the menu. Luna rolled her eyes. "We're going to have to get the cheese curds, aren't we?"

My mouth dropped open in fake shock. "What? You don't want cheese curds? That's it, this is over."

Luna laughed softly. "Okay, but we should also get calamari. Only getting cheese at a seafood restaurant is a travesty."

"You won't get any complaints from me." I looked over the other offerings. "I'm getting the jumbo sea scallop pasta, you?"

She sighed. "I'm worried that no matter what I'll be disappointed. But I guess I'll get the salmon Florentine."

After reading over our choices, I closed the menu. "I think we should head to a local ice cream shop for dessert. We could even call the others and bring something home. Have a party."

Her mouth twitched. "Maybe. We can discuss that at the end."

The server came and we ordered. Then I turned to Luna. "As much as it's fun to pretend you invited me to dinner because of me, I'm guessing you have an ulterior motive." I sipped my water, curious as to what she'd say.

"I thought we could start to figure out this thing we have where we pass images and words." Her mouth squeezed shut. "It's supposed to be secret, right? Something with alphas? Mates even?"

"Yeah, I think all alphas have a bit of it, but mates can do more. And from what I've been told, what we did before you even agreed to be an alpha means our connection is really strong."

"Okay, so let's see what we can do. Is it just images, or can we do words? Just words, or full sentences? Do we have to touch?"

My eyes widened. "You want to train this, don't you? Like what Dad does."

I could see her trying to roll her eyes, but she was smiling too wide. "Maybe. I was even thinking, after we test this out a bit, we could set up a meeting with your dad and get this really figured out. It seems like a major advantage."

Something between excitement and happiness bubbled within me. Despite that, I tried to keep my voice calm. "I'm sure he'd be willing to help."

Luna made a face at me before she laughed. "I can almost hear him cheering now."

"Okay, let's start. I'm going to send you an image. Let me know what you get."

She narrowed her eyes, then nodded.

The table next to us had a man and a woman. The man was surrounded by a red aura, he was strong-willed and confident. Swirling in his base pigment were a darker red and orange. He was feeling aggressive.

The woman's base color was purple, she was more intuitive or empathic. Zipping within her base aura were swirls of blues and purple. The blues alone would be distraction or grief, a variation of disapproval. Add purple—boredom, disgust, loathing—and she was feeling a bit of remorse as well.

If I were to guess, this date wasn't going to end well.

I tried to send not only the static image of the couple, but the movement of the secondary colors. I really wanted Luna to see how fast the purple and the darker blue moved within the woman's aura as well as the lighter orange. This couple was really having two different dates.

A moment after I sent the image, Luna's eyes widened. "Holy ... gods. Is that ... are those? Pebble, is *that* what my mom has gone on and on about for years?"

When I'd decided to send that image, it hadn't occurred to me that this was something Luna had heard about her whole life and had never seen. "Yeah, those are auras. It's what I see around everyone ... *all* the time."

Luna closed her eyes. "Can you ... I don't know, look around the restaurant and send me more?"

Does she regret not having this ability? Is she beginning to understand her mom more?

"Of course."

For the next few minutes, I looked at different tables and sent Luna what I saw. Sometimes she asked me if her interpretation of the auras were correct. *'That couple is in love, right? They both have yellow and green in their auras. And he has some greenish blue.'*

'Turquoise,' I interrupted, a small smile tugging up the side of my mouth. Switching over to teacher mode helped me to flesh out my understanding of auras in a way that study alone wouldn't.

'Oh, yeah, right. Turquoise. But my interpretation is correct, right?'

I smiled, sipping my water. *'It is.'* I moved my gaze to a different table, one with kids.

Luna snorted. *'How much do you want to bet that table is not having fun? The older kids, with the dark purple. That's contempt, right? A combination of red and purple? Combining boredom and disgust of purple and annoyance and anger of red. Then the dad, I'm assuming the dad, has aggression and the mom disapproval. Then the younger kid is all love and optimism. I can't imagine where her emotions come from.'*

It took all my effort not to react.

Our appetizers came, and I stopped projecting to Luna. I realized my hands shook from the effort of our connection. "Damn, I don't know why I did all of that before we'd eaten."

Across from me, Luna's eyes snapped open. She reached over and popped a cheese curd in her mouth and moaned. "I hate how good these are."

My smile almost hurt my cheeks. We ate for a few minutes before I paused and leaned forward, squinting at her.

She glared back. "What? Do I have something in my teeth?"

"No, it's just ... when we did ... you know." I vaguely waved at the tables around us. "Were we talking out loud?"

Luna's fork full of tasty calamari froze halfway to her mouth, which was hanging open.

Chapter 15 – Power Struggle

Tuesday morning Luna, Dayna, and I laughed about the wolf in my tour group. Dayna had asked if anything interesting had happened during the tours while the three of us had our morning coffee.

"You were worried about a teen girl who's ... what? Half your size?"

My chin dropped and I gazed down at my petite body. "I'm not that big."

"No, but you work out regularly. You're strong. You took out two wolves by yourself. I doubt that girl and her mom could put the drop on you if they took you by surprise." The citrusy amusement flowed from Luna as she smirked at me with one eyebrow raised.

"Fine, you're right. But it's a good precedent to be in."

Next to Luna, Dayna laughed. "You're not wrong. And in the end, I personally would rather you call in Tanner than take on the big bad baby wolf and her mom, even though you did have Conner there, too."

It was too much, and I laughed.

Conner came in. "Getting coffee. Anyone need a refill?"

Luna and I held up our mugs. He chuckled. "Do you two know how similar you can be at times?"

A growl bubbled up from my gut and I saw Luna glaring at him. He just laughed more, filling our coffees, and bringing them back to us.

"Pebble, how long did it take for you to get used to the echoes of people in your head?" Luna began to rub her forehead.

A stillness came over my body as I contemplated her question. *Have I gotten used to it?* "I think I'm still adjusting, but I did call and get advice from the California alphas a couple of times. To be honest, I've been kind of wondering if you'd ask."

Next to Luna, Dayna tilted her head. "If you have connections to all of us in your head, does that mean you can talk to us mentally? Find us, and—I don't know—do other things?"

The pack held behind the mental fence seemed to take more of my mental space, as if they knew they were being discussed. I rubbed my temples, trying to soothe my head. "I can't talk to anyone." I thought about the previous night with Luna, but that was a big secret. "Well, no one but Conner, but that's because he's epsilon. And he can mostly only do that because they're part of the pack. As for what we can do, we can get a general direction ... if I really focus on a single wolf, I may be able to pinpoint where that person is. It's not a guarantee."

After a moment, Dayna turned to Conner. "What about you? Can you find a pack wolf?"

His face scrunched up. "Maybe eventually. Jade has been training me, but this is all so new. Finding the connections has been tricky. I'm hoping to visit California this summer for a few weeks to get more training. Fern will probably head out there, too. We both feel it'll be good for us."

I shook my head. "Why all these questions?"

"Trista. Isn't she still part of the pack? I've been thinking about it since she didn't show for the run last week. Tanner and Clare have been in and out of here a lot, wanting to find her. Could you help with that?"

Her question had merit.

Leaning back, I held my coffee mug close to my nose and breathed deep, letting the heady scent fill me. Then I closed my eyes and imagined the pack in my mind. I looked for the connection to Trista, the echo of her wolf in the group of wolves and their emotions I held, connecting them to me, making them part of my pack. As happened the last few times, at first, I couldn't see her.

Did she leave Wisconsin? Did she break her link to me? Can she do that without my knowledge? Would I have felt it? There were so many questions to ask the other alphas.

It took a few ... moments? Minutes? Hours? It was hard to tell when I was playing in my mind. But, eventually, I found the connection to the traitorous woman. There was a block there, as if she worked to keep me away. *I really need to talk to Mom!*

I held my hand out to Conner. "Can you see her?"

His voice sounded soft, far off. "I can't. Can you start with someone less ... prickly?"

I laughed, then focused on Piper. Through our connection where I held his hand, I could feel his muscles relax. "Okay ... yeah. I can see her. She's ... that way."

Dayna's voice filled the void. "He's pointing towards the front door."

"Okay, so, let's try Trista again." I focused on Trista.

Conner grunted with effort. The muscles in his arm tensed, but in the end, nothing. Whatever she did to block me worked on both of us.

Wednesday, I had two more tours. This time, Conner didn't show up and neither did any other wayward wolf. It was just parents, teens, and lots of questions about Madison, the campus, and if it was always this cold.

The tours were in the morning and afternoon. As long as the day was, it gave me time alone to have lunch downtown, and I was home by late afternoon. As soon as I got into the living room, I collapsed on one of the couches.

My muscles had just begun to relax when the front door opened and Tanner came in, followed by Tyler. They both sat in recliners across from me. My first instinct was to say, "No. Anything can wait until tomorrow." But I knew that wasn't true. So, instead, I forced myself to sit up and give the two men a wary smile.

Tanner leaned on his knees, his purple aura showing his base nature strong with intuition—*no wonder he's good at his job*—swirled with fast moving steel blue, mixed with an orangish yellow. He was pensive and optimistic. "One of the trackers activated. We know where she is right now. She may not keep whatever she moved on her for long. We have to act fast."

Though every muscle in my body protested, I shot to my feet, a snarl in my voice. "I'm going with."

"No. That's not your job." Tanner's voice was hard and his eyes glowed. His aura shot through with a lighter blue ... disapproval.

He wouldn't scare me. "I'm strong, Tanner. I have power. Don't keep me from this. She played me for a fool for months and I'm going to see this through to the end."

He snarled, his face tight. "I don't like this." He enunciated each word. "If I bring you along, it's under heavy protest."

"That's fine," I snapped back. "Now, let's go before Tyler loses the signal."

We ended up meeting Easton in the arboretum not far from the pack house. It felt like a trap of some sort.

Easton narrowed his eyes at me, then shot his dad the same look. Tanner held up his hands, and hissed out in a low voice, "She's alpha. You try fighting with her."

With an exaggerated sigh, Easton said, "Will you at least go in as a wolf? You'll be more dangerous that way."

I wanted to snap at him, but in the end, it *was* their operation, and he wasn't wrong.

Both Tyler and I wolfed out. Tanner knelt. "While you two shifted, I scoped out the area. Trista and two men are in a wooded area about a half-mile to the southwest. I want you two to flank the group. Tyler, if you can manage, get further behind them. Easton and I will engage, see if we can get answers. You two are our backup."

Once the plans were in place, we all headed out. We hadn't gone more than a few steps towards our target when we all sensed a dog to our right. Tensing, my head snapped to try to get a better scent of the situation. The others, all between me and the canine, mirrored my motions.

"Spot! Don't get too far ahead of us!" The woman's voice was distant. I could barely hear it.

A low snarl bubbled in my gut. The last thing we needed was innocent people or animals stumbling in on this confrontation.

Eyes narrowed, I gazed up at Tanner.

His face was tight as he searched first my eyes and then Tyler's. "Right, distraction. Tyler. You have the least battle training of the four of us, and you're in wolf form. I also fear what our fearless leader will do if I try to send her off. Go, get the dog chasing you, or chase it off. Get the norms going in any direction but towards us. Then either find us or meet us back at the cars."

The wolf's head bobbed once before he bounded off.

Once we heard the joyous sound of the chase, Tanner turned to me. "Same directions. Flank the group. I want you as backup."

I wanted to snarl but agreed.

The snow on the ground was cold under my paws, but it provided a barrier to dead leaves and twigs that would betray my presence. I moved as silently as I could, sniffing the air until I caught Trista's scent and that of the other two people. Three wolves, all in our territory.

There was a wide tree that had grown out in two directions, the trunk split into a V shape about a foot and half above ground level. I slunk behind it. I could just hear the others speaking.

"You're still part of the pack. Why did you stop engaging with them? That totally messed things up. I know we left you here for a couple of weeks, Beth, but how dumb are you? You didn't run during their moon run. Do you want to get caught?"

Trista ... Beth, squawked in frustration. "You don't understand. Jade was in town and talking to that traitorous scum. I saw Quinn. He had to have seen me. There is no way he didn't report who I was to Pebble and the rest of them. I couldn't take that chance. If I'd gone back, they would've killed me."

The male who had spoken first continued. "There's no way Quinn could've identified you that quickly. You messed everything up for no reason. You said that you and Pebble were like best friends. Even if the idiot *had* seen you, I bet you could've played it off. Convinced her of some story. You said you had her wrapped around your pinky."

"But her phone. I had it at the apartment, and now it's gone." Beth all but stomped her foot.

The second male snorted. "I've seen your place, Beth. It's a mess." The condescension dripped, as if he spoke to a child. "It probably fell into the pit of despair you call a floor. Clean up once in a while, then when you find the damn thing you'll realize ghosting that pack was the most idiotic thing you could've done."

"Fine. I'll go home, clean. And when I *don't* find it, you'll apologize." She crossed her arms over her chest, agitated.

"And when you do?"

She sniffed as if that were impossible. "I'll fix it. Pebble is so desperate for friends, she's an easy mark. A phone call or two and I'll be back on dating terms with her. I'll have her eating out of my hands."

Bile rose in the back of my throat at her words. *Did she actually think we'd been dating? We had a couple of meals together, but that was as friends, pack mates. That was it. Dating? Gross.*

"Good," the first guy said. "Then we can poison her."

Tanner stepped out of the trees, slow clapping. "Wow, it's like dinner and a show, but there's no food, and the show is awful." He chuckled. "You all are really bad at this, you know that?"

A tension ran through the group, and Beth squealed, voice high, "How are you here?"

The boys just snickered as they rolled their eyes at Tanner. "You call us dumb? It's one against three. Looks like the one who can't count is the real dunce." And then they both ran at Tanner.

Nothing about what I saw said Tanner needed help.

Then Tris ... Beth bent and pulled a knife out of her boot. Easton ran from the woods and tackled her. I watched as he squeezed her wrist. She twisted and bucked, but Easton held her down, squeezing, until she released the knife.

There was a grunt, and I turned to Tanner as he and one of the two men dropped to the ground. He rolled, got to his feet, and ran towards me.

I heard a crack and saw, as Easton stood, Beth's lifeless form still on the ground.

A shiver ran down my spine, but I focused on the wolf coming my way, Tanner following. As he neared, I released a bit of my mantle, not enough to reach any of the others in the field, but enough to remind me of who I was. The man stumbled when he felt my power, and I leapt up, taking him down. As we fell, I tore out his throat with my teeth.

He landed hard, and I used the snow on the ground to clear out my mouth.

Tanner approached and made sure the man wouldn't rise. "Quick and efficient, just like training." His grunt of approval pleased me more than I would want to admit. He continued—not that I could've responded in wolf form. "I'd have rather you not be involved, boss." He waved and continued before he could've heard my low growl. "I know, you're all grown up, and alpha, but you have to understand, a part of me still wants to protect that innocent five-year-old girl we found on the side of I80. After years of not wanting to even hunt a rabbit, my instinct is to shield you from this. That said, your swift action was well executed."

Though part of his words rankled the alpha within me, they also helped counter the queasy feeling I had from killing a man. There was a reason for the years of training Dad insisted on.

Easton tried to keep the last man alive so we'd have someone to question, but he pulled a knife before his hand was fully secured. Their grappling ended in his death.

Tanner turned to me, his face tight with frustration. "Go, change. I'll be right there."

I took a moment to gaze around the small glade. This was an aspect of being alpha. Though part of me felt guilty that I let others do my job, an equal amount of guilty niggled in about my happiness that I didn't have to deal with the cleanup. Shaking myself, a tremor ran down my body as I turned and ran towards the car.

Halfway there, my stomach turned and emptied. I'd seen death many times, even human death, but this was the first time I'd gone into a situation with it being the final goal.

Quivers of unease snaked through my body. I made my way to the car and laid down. Once I felt the quakes stop, I told my wolf it was time to let my humanity out. It was time to face the world and the decisions I'd made on two feet.

By the time I was human and dressed, the others were back, including Tyler, who had also shifted.

Easton and Tyler looked at me uncertainly, but Tanner's gaze held respect. "You did good out there, alpha."

"I didn't do enough. I shouldn't have left you at the end." My voice was soft, weaker than I liked.

"That's what we're here for. Alphas don't do clean up. You don't even have to do all the take downs. Talk to your parents, or to the California pack. Next time, stay home and let us do our jobs. But in the end, you faced your fears and didn't turn away from the uglier side of what we do. It's not easy, but you did it." He spoke clearly as he stared at me with intention. He wanted me to hear his words.

"Does this mean it's over?"

A smile spread across Easton's face. "When we were at Trista's place, she had a list of all the people who'd come to Madison. We found their IDs. Based on that note, yes. This is all of them."

A sense of wonder overtook me. "It seems too easy." Then, excitement washed through me. "But now I can call Mom and Dad. It's actually over."

We got into the cars, and I pulled out my phone and tapped on Mom's contact. "Hiya, sweetie, how are you? Ready for school next week? I can't believe I won't be there."

I wanted to laugh at how normal that all sounded. "Yes, I'm ready, and I am ... I don't know how I am. I'm in a car with Tyler and Tanner, so they can hear you ... just so you know."

"Hi, boys."

They both said 'hi,' though Tanner's sounded more like a grunt.

"So, why did you call?" I could hear a door closing behind her.

"Well, we're leaving the arboretum. We just finished cleaning out the last of the lone wolves. Mom ... it's over." Part of me wanted to tell her to come home, but I knew it wasn't that easy.

I could hear Dad cheering in the background. "Way to go, Applesauce."

Closer, Mom said, "Well, now all we need to do is find alphas to take over here. The old alphas encouraged dominance fights so much within this pack that all the really strong wolves left or eliminated each other in the fights. All we've been doing is trying to teach tolerance and peace to wolves that have lived with tension and fear for years. Everyone is weak and scared. The old pack members have no desire to return. I know not all packs are as calm as ours, but I believe living with an epsilon really did more than we knew."

Chapter 16 – Back To The Grind

When Tanner dropped me off, all I wanted to do was hide in my room and sleep. I knew we'd just accomplished something huge, but at the same time, the day had been long, and I needed some time to decompress.

There was a knock at my door, and I grumbled, really not wanting to talk to anyone. Realizing it could be another emergency, I sighed and sat up. "Yeah, come in." My voice sounded flat.

Luna walked in carrying a chocolate shake. "Tanner's in the kitchen. He made this and told me to bring it to you. I was just going to come talk but he said you hadn't eaten enough and this would help."

I had perked up at the chocolate shake and only listened to about half of what she'd said. "Oh! Gimme!" I held my hands out like a toddler, opening and closing my fingers excitedly.

She held it out and rolled her eyes. "Gods above, you're the alpha of a werewolf pack, Pebble. Act like it."

"Have you tasted one of Tanner's shakes?"

"You're kidding, right? Nothing is that good."

Though it hurt my soul, I tilted the glass to her and raised an eyebrow. She grunted and took the offered sweet, drinking a bit. Her eyes bulged and her mouth dropped open. "Holy ... what does he put in this? Is it even legal?"

"Give it back and no one gets hurt."

Luna's eyes narrowed and she took another drink before handing it over. I growled low, then scooted back on my bed until I could lean against the wall. "Why were you coming to talk with me?"

"You left with Tanner, who was feeling stressed and tense. Then Allison texted me asking why you were so upset. We're partners and I want to know what happened. I get that you may not want everyone to know, but Pebble, I need to know."

My head hit the wall hard enough to make a loud banging sound. She wasn't wrong, but reliving the afternoon would suck. Before I could say anything, she tilted her head. "Can you send me images? Would that be easier?"

I shook my head. "They wouldn't be pretty."

"How about a combination? Speed up the process."

I let the chocolate shake settle me as I sent a series of images to Luna. It started with my collapse on the couch after the tour and ended when Tanner walked into the field. I added mental commentary when I felt it was needed.

Despite us getting closer, I left out the part about my tearing out someone's throat with my teeth. Not only did I not want to relive it—a shiver ran down my back—I wasn't sure what Luna would think of me if she knew.

"Please tell me none of those idiots made it out of the arboretum." The snarl in her voice blanketed me in a peace I hadn't realized I needed. She'd also moved to sit next to me at some point, her hand on my thigh.

How did I miss that?

"No, that's why I stopped. The fighting got gruesome."

A smile played at the side of her mouth. "I bet. Tanner is fierce and his son doesn't seem to be far behind him."

I just nodded. I went to take another sip and realized I'd finished the shake. "Let's go get more. Maybe Tanner will make one for you."

"Or," she said, sliding her gaze to me, "we could have the dinner Conner is making first. It smells divine."

Once I opened the door, the smell of steak and potatoes that permeated the air overtook all other scents and my body trembled with need. Even after the shake, I hadn't realized how hungry I was.

In the kitchen, Tanner smiled. "Good, I was hoping I wouldn't have to carry you out for dinner."

Luna waggled her brows. "She was catching me up on the afternoon. Telling me about Trista and her crew."

Easton smiled, practically bouncing. "I'm so glad this is over. Are we going to have a full pack meeting, or will you just send out a blast email? I mean, we need to tell everyone about how you bullied Dad into letting you come on the operation and took out one of the creeps yourself."

Next to me, Luna stiffened. Tanner's eyes narrowed. "Ah, she didn't tell you that part. Pebble doesn't tend to brag very much, but yes, one ran, and she eliminated him."

Until that moment, I hadn't realized the degree to which I cared what Luna thought about me and the actions I took as alpha of the pack. What if this disgusted her? Sure, she was protective of the people she called her own ... but to the death? Would she think less of me if she knew I was able to kill and come home this calmly? Was that even possible? We'd just started to form ... something. Steeling myself as I realized the true heart of my issues, I tried to steady myself. What if this made her want to leave?

Barely breathing, I focused hard on the far side of the counter. All my muscles had tensed, and I just wanted to go back to my room and curl up on my bed. *Would this day ever end?*

After a few seconds, Luna's arm slid across my shoulders. She leaned down and kissed my cheek, then she whispered softly in my ear, "Good job, I'm proud of you."

With a sigh, all my muscles released.

I wanted to forget the battle from Wednesday night. I'd sent out an email, deciding we'd had enough pack meetings for one winter break. Another part of me wanted to party to celebrate the end of the lone wolves in under a month.

In the end, the pack took the option out of my hands. On Friday night, a group of us, mostly those of us heading off to college, Tanner, Easton, and Tyler, went out to a big dinner at a burger joint. Everyone had burgers, fries, sodas ... or shakes, and generally a good time.

The meal was to celebrate overcoming a dangerous situation as a pack with new alphas. It was also a last meal before several of us moved into the dorms on Saturday. Spring semester was about to begin.

Easton started in on his first burger. "So, all of you are moving out to live in the dorms?"

The chocolate shake I'd ordered helped as a palate cleanser between my burger and fries. I took a long sip, the thick concoction fighting the straw, before answering. It wasn't as good as Tanner's, but what was? "Yeah.

Having to drive back and forth isn't ideal, and we all have rooms. I'm planning on spending part of my time at home, so the den isn't empty. The idea of it all alone makes me sad."

Tanner pointed a fry at me. "I would agree if you were moving into the dorms for the full semester, but if you're doing half time at both locations, I think it'll be fine."

"Yeah," Luna added. "And Dayna and I will be in and out, too."

"Me, too," added Conner.

"You know," Easton said. "I have no problem with my apartment being empty for a bit. I can move into pack house until things are figured out."

Everyone looked at him, and I felt the warmth that only pack could bring.

Saturday morning, after I dropped my stuff off in the room, I had to give another tour. I only had one to give, but it was frustrating not having the rest of the day to settle in. When I got to the dorm, it didn't look like Hollis had arrived yet.

I just wanted to move in and double check where all my pack members were, not worry about my job. As I headed to the Union, I quickly texted everyone and made sure they were situated in their rooms and everything was okay. With new animals, the scents of the dorms could be an issue. They all promised to keep me informed if there was a problem.

After I checked on the group text to members who could go furry, I shot off another to Fern. Hollis had said they were okay with me moving in, but I was still worried. If Fern saw Hollis, they'd make sure she was okay with sharing a dorm room with me. As much as I didn't want to commute, I would live at home to save my friendship.

There were so many students and their parents milling about campus that the tour was a whole new experience. It took an extra bit of time as we had to navigate cars and move in carts. There were mobs of students near Library Mall heading to the bookstore and the Union. By the time I got done and sent my clients off, I was ready for a nap.

Back in the dorm room, Hollis stepped towards me, then stumbled back, almost like she wanted to give me a hug. Finally, she settled on a shy smile. "Hiya, Pebble. I saw your stuff but didn't know where you went."

The aborted hug disappointed me, but I understood. We were still navigating something new. "I was scheduled to give a tour." I let one of my eyebrows jump to my hairline to let her know my opinion of my day's activities.

Her jaw dropped. "God, that sounds awful. How bad of a maze was that?"

Her indignation and animated disbelief amused me, and I smiled, a bit of joy filling me. I laughed at the memory and told her a couple of horror stories of the insanity of students moving in and the parents 'helping.'

We sat on the edge of our beds, and it started to feel like old times.

It almost made the experience worth it ... almost.

By Monday morning, we were grumbling about the bad coffee and mediocre food, ready to trudge to class in a welcoming snow storm, and it felt like our friendship was mending.

It didn't take long to get into a routine. Unlike in the fall, I didn't have classes on Fridays. Each day, I started off with Spanish. It was a struggle, but since Hollis was a genius at the language, I could always get her help. That was my only session on Monday, so I could get studying done if need be. Tuesdays and Thursdays, I had Folklore and Communication Arts scheduled. Both Fern and Hollis had signed up for the Gen Ed courses. When we'd walked in, I had been surprised to see Dayna and Luna in Folklore as well.

My last credits were filled with an online psych class on human-animal interactions. I was stupidly excited about the it, though not as excited about the format.

Most of my time was filled up in the morning, so if it was needed, I could head home in the afternoon ... or sit and study in the Electric Brew, my favorite coffee house.

When my boss learned I had Fridays off, she scheduled me to give a tour every morning. At the end of the second week of the semester, after I'd given a tour, Hollis found me at the corner table of the Electric Brew, enjoying coffee and a ham and cheese croissant. "Hi, Pebble. Can I join you?"

I could only hear her clearly over the music and talking of the other people because of my excellent werewolf senses. Nodding, I waved my hand at the other seat.

Instead of sitting, she tossed her bag, then went to order something for herself. When she returned, she had coffee and two chocolate chip cookies. They steamed, and each one was huge, the size of the saucer they sat on. "I got one for you. Figured you needed a chocolate fix. How was the tour?"

My full answer was a dramatic roll of my eyes and a huge bite of the cookie.

She chuckled, leaning close to talk. "Do you need the job?"

I sighed. "Probably not. I thought it would be a good way to get more of a college experience, but now it just feels like it takes up time I'd rather have to do other things."

"Like rule the world?" Hollis winked and bit into her own cookie.

"Yep, that's me, megalomaniac at your command."

Hollis bobbed her head. "That's what I wanted to talk to you about, actually."

A chill tickled my body. *Did I do something wrong in the last two weeks?* "Um ... okay. What's up?"

She released a held breath. "It's not ... I mean, don't worry. I just." She clasped the warm mug of coffee in both of her hands and lifted it up to her face. After breathing deeply, she sipped, then placed the mug down. "Do you remember that night ... you know, when you, me, and Fern went out to dinner?"

With slow deliberation, I nodded. "It would be hard to forget it. It was the night so many things in my life changed. My best friend in the world started being afraid of me, and another friend ... well, I learned a lot about Fern after that."

A humorless laugh erupted from Hollis. "As you drifted from me, you got closer to them."

"Trust me, Hollis. I was dragged from you, kicking and screaming." I reached across the table and wrapped her hands in mine. "All I've ever wanted since that day was to have our relationship go back to how it was."

"To have me ignorant of who you are?" She spoke down to our hands.

My shoulders slumped. "Yes and no. If we can be how we were before with you knowing, then I'm all for that. I just want you to be my best friend again. I miss you so much, you don't even understand."

"Okay, well, I have an idea."

Every muscle in my body tensed. Thoughts swirled, but I couldn't fathom what she could be talking about. "What are you thinking?"

She licked her lips. "The only—" she leaned in to whisper, "—werewolf I've ever seen was that one who tried to bite me. That awful one you ..." She just waved her hand and sat back, mouth shut tight.

I mirrored her posture, leaning back and sipping my coffee. "Okay, and? What are you thinking, Hollis?"

"I'm scared, Pebble. What if ... what if you showed me one that wasn't scary?"

Both my brows flew up. What she wanted wasn't unreasonable. It actually made sense. "Okay. Why not? We could even do it tomorrow. Either at my place or at the zoo; we have a training spot there."

"Really? Like, that's it? You don't have to ask anyone?"

I smirked. "I'm the alpha. People ask me."

Chapter 17 – Place In The Pack

Friday afternoon, Fern and I convinced Hollis to spend the night at pack house with us. It would make showing her my wolf on Saturday morning easier. As I packed my school bag—I definitely had homework—I updated the message group I'd set up for me, Luna, Dayna, Conner, and Fern. Though I mentioned Hollis joining us, I didn't mention why. If they wanted to know, they could come home this weekend.

My next text was to Easton, letting him know of our plans, and seeing if he was able to pick us up. If not, we'd arrange something else. He said he was out on patrol, and we were on our own.

Next was arranging a ride with Uber.

We all sat in the living room, Hollis and Fern on the couch, and me on one of the love seats. Hollis kept looking around. "This place is so big. I mean, I've been here, but we usually just go to your room and then back out to the car. I don't think we've ever just sat in here to talk. I've never really thought about it. Do you ever get lost?"

The whole idea of her being here made me nervous and giddy. "Not since I was a kid. And then I just pretended I was playing hide and go seek."

I tried to keep my face neutral as her eyes widened. "Really?"

"Yeah, I think the adults were more traumatized by those events than me."

Hollis's gaze kept boring into me until I started to laugh, then she threw a pillow at my head. "God, Pebble, you're awful."

Fern chuckled. The two sat close and a vanilla scent surrounded them—delight and pleasure. It settled something in me that they were building their relationship again. Smirking, Fern said, "I don't know, it was kind of funny. Can you imagine five-year-old Pebble sitting under the table in the library, paging through a book while half the adults in the pack searched frantically for her?"

This time the ginger scent of shock emanated from Hollis and her jaw dropped ... not the reaction Fern probably expected. "This place has a library? Are you kidding me? And you said it *isn't* that big? What other fancy rooms does it have?"

My mouth opened and shut a few times, but I didn't have much of an answer for her accusation. "I mean, there isn't a pool or anything."

"But there is a gym," Fern mumbled.

I groaned, sinking into my seat. "Are you trying to help?"

"No, not really. This is pretty fun to watch honestly." Their smile kept getting bigger.

Hollis stood. "That's it. Full tour. I've known you longer than just about anyone. I deserve to see this place in all its glory." Her hand waved in a huge arc as she said 'all.'

We spent the next forty or so minutes walking around the house. Unlike most new people, Hollis poked around as if she were interested in buying the place. "Can you imagine the blanket forts we could've built in here?"

Trying to see the library with all its tables and chairs with a new sense of purpose, I relented. "We'd have had to sneak a lot of blankets up, this was considered an adult area. I mean, it wouldn't have been impossible."

Between us, Fern shook their head. "You said that this was a food free zone, or at least highly discouraged." They stepped forward and slowly spun, looking around as if casing the joint. "I'd vote for any forts to be made in the basement. There's a kitchen down there. Much better access."

I narrowed my eyes and debated. "I mean, yeah. But then you have to invite way more people. It's more private up here. And," I paused for dramatic effect, "books!"

We all laughed, and I could feel the walls that the attack had created erode even more. The Three Musketeers were becoming a trio again.

Scents from the kitchen started to fill the air; garlicky meat made my stomach growl with approval.

By the time we got done and back to the kitchen, Luna, Dayna, and Conner were there. Even better, Conner was cooking.

I was happy the others were here. Being surrounded by pack made my soul feel complete and centered. My friends were great, but other wolves were better. It wasn't until Hollis froze, glaring at Luna, that I realized how many of my opinions and feelings had changed.

"What are you doing here?" Hollis snapped out, her voice low and cold.

I placed a hand on her arm. "They're pack Hollis, they have every right to be here. It's their home, too."

She shook her head. "No, this is *your* home."

There was always something new to uncover and explain. One day something would be easy ... right? "No.

Well ... yes, it is. But it's more than that. This is the den to the Wisconsin werewolf pack. Usually the alphas live here, though it isn't necessary. I do plan to live here." I bit my lip. In the few weeks since Luna had become a wolf, we had never discussed any of this. I wasn't sure how new any of this topic was to her either.

While I spoke, Luna's face had scrunched up into an expression I recognized, though hadn't seen for a while. "And if you hadn't heard, I'm one of the alphas. I have as much right to be here as Pebble. The only person who doesn't have a right," one of her brows shot up to her hairline, "is you."

Every muscle in Hollis's body tensed. Her shoulders rose towards her ears, and she scowled. "How dare you? I've been Pebble's friend, supporting her since I met her. What have you done? Huh? Nothing but be a—"

Dayna slipped between them, putting a hand on Luna's shoulder. "Both of you stop."

Her words started my brain, and I stepped forward. "Hollis, you are my sister, and I love you, but Luna is right, she has every right to be here. This is the pack home."

"But she's been so mean to you—to us." The misery in her look as she swung to me, desperate for understanding, cut deep.

"In the past." As I spoke, Fern stepped in behind Hollis, wrapping their arms around her. "Things have changed. I know we've talked about a lot of things, but this is really important for you to understand. I don't know Luna's final plans, we haven't really discussed them. But this *is* pack house, the den for all the Wisconsin werewolves. As for Conner and Dayna, it would be easier while they're in college to live here. Once they graduate ... who knows. Though, I'm starting to form a theory ... but I need to talk with Jade and my parents about that first."

Dayna shook her head. "Talk about a teaser. Maybe you should tell us your thoughts, and we can help you to figure it out."

"Maybe." I relented. "Let me think about it." The scents filling the air made my stomach growl and I realized we had the perfect distraction. "Conner, what are you making?"

He shot a satisfied smile over his shoulder. "Pork chops, garlic mashed potatoes, and a salad. Well, Luna *was* making a salad before you distracted her."

"What?" She shrugged. "I didn't think you wanted me to cut myself while chopping a cucumber."

Dayna pushed her away from the cutting board. "Gods above, woman. I'll make the salad, you go sit. You are a terror in here."

"I can make salad ... usually." Though she argued her ability, she sashayed to sit at the table.

"No, go." Dayna sighed dramatically as she began to chop with a skill I knew I'd never have.

Once seated, Luna narrowed her eyes at the group. "Now, as for where we all end up living," she shot Hollis a glance as if daring her to start up her arguments again, "I don't know."

"What, you don't want to live in this five-star luxury home?" Conner's brows bobbed up and down at her.

She quirked a smile at him. "It's not that ... I just hadn't thought about it. I mean, Pebble's parents *are* returning, right?"

Everyone in the room turned to me. My mind momentarily went blank, and I had no idea what to say. Then I felt Fern's hand gently rub my back and I remembered to breathe. *Right, my parents. I can answer something about this.* "To be honest, I don't know. They should be coming back when they find new alphas to take over the Tennessee pack. That's the plan, but they can't seem to find anyone willing to take over for them."

Despite my calm words, my hands started to tremble. *Did Luna not want to be an alpha of this pack? Was she hoping that all of this was a band-aid to tide the pack over? Didn't she understand that one day my parents wanted to retire?*

Feeling a bit dizzy, I sat at one of the counter stools, then licked my lips. "Just to be clear, my parents were hoping to retire from being alphas after I graduated college, or, after me and the other alpha, whenever that person was found, graduated. They are hoping to find a permanent replacement. Luna, you do know they believe that person to be you, right?"

Luna's face tightened and she slowly leaned back. "Yes, but I also know you said I didn't *have* to take this gig. If I wanted to, I could return home and remain part of the gaggle I grew up in."

It felt like each word she said clawed into me, drawing blood. "Yeah. You're right. I did." My voice sounded soft and far away to me. I tried to sound nonchalant, but I feared I failed. "The major dilemma has passed, and though you hold the mantle right now, you can decide you don't want it. Nothing has to be a lifetime sentence."

One side of Luna's mouth quirked up. "Okay, just checking. I haven't made any final decisions. This has all happened really fast. Six weeks ago, the idea of becoming a wolf wasn't on my radar. Now, you're talking about me living in this house for the rest of my life. I mean, you'd allow Dayna to be here too, and she's always been my best friend, but it's a lot to think about, and I don't want to leap without thinking."

A mug of herbal tea was placed on the counter. I looked up to see Conner giving me a wry smile. I mouthed 'thank you' then took a sip, letting the warm essence soothe me.

Hollis sat next to me. "This has been ... interesting. Are you sure tomorrow is a good idea? Everything seems so ... intense."

I snorted. "Yeah. Showing you my wolf will be fine. Nothing to worry about." I forced myself to chuckle.

Dayna smiled wide, eyes twinkling. "You're here to see animals?"

"Yeah. I thought maybe if I saw Pebble's wolf, I'd be less scared."

Luna scoffed. "I don't know why you're scared in the first place. The animal is just us ... in animal form. Nothing to fear. If you're fine with the human, then why worry about the animal?" And ... her snappish nature was back. So much for the few moments of peace.

"Maybe because she was attacked by a wolf?" Fern said low, their voice cutting through all the tension in the room. "Luna, you need to be more willing to allow others to feel things you don't, especially if you're going to be alpha."

"Isn't that what this whole conversation has been about? Maybe I don't *want* to be alpha," she snapped back, eyes narrowing on the three of us.

It was Fern's turn to scoff, undeterred by the bite in Luna's voice. "And maybe you're scared. Scared for the first time in your life. You have the chance to be part of something big and beautiful. A group that is so much larger than just you. You're worried you won't be enough, you'll mess up, you'll fail. Well, Luna, that's life. If you can't realize you're a flawed human being, the same as the rest of us, you'll live a lonely, miserable existence."

Luna's eyes narrowed. "You don't know me nearly as well as you think, Fern. I'm not afraid of anything. If I want to do something, I do it, and I'll be the best. Don't think for one second my hesitation is due to fear."

Again, Dayna moved to stand between the two that were arguing and put out her hands. *Has this been her role her whole life? Stepping between Luna and her targets?* "Enough. Fern, give Luna room to maneuver, this is a big decision and it's hers. Pebble has had her whole life to figure this out."

"No, I haven't. I've had just over a year. But you're right, it *isn't* a decision to be made lightly."

After a moment, Dayna nodded then turned to Luna. "And you. Stop snapping at everyone. Especially if your path is heading toward a life-long leadership role. You need to control your anger and yourself. Be a role model to those around you. We've discussed this."

Luna's upper lip just twitched. "Whatever."

Before anyone could say anything else, there was a stabbing pain in my head. I groaned and let the premonition play out.

I was pulling ... something. Luna was there, helping me. No, she was pulling away from me. Of course she was. Could she ever work with me? *Struggling, she went off in a different direction, suddenly there was an explosion, but it wasn't an explosion, because it was only gas? A gas bomb, but there was an animal by Luna's feet.* Was that a cat?

My head shot up and I saw everyone gaping at me. As the remnants of the images faded, a sense of sadness washed through me. *Does this mean she's really going to leave? All this ... time, work, connection, and it's all for nothing?*

Fern touched my back. "Are you okay? Was that a ..."

The connection of pack jerked me out of my maudlin thoughts, and I shivered. Slowly, I gazed up into their eyes, then licked my lips. "Yeah, it was."

One of Dad's strategies involved immediately talking out my vision. Though I didn't have anyone who had experience in deciphering my premonitions, any assistance would help. I explained to them what I saw.

Dayna smiled. "One day Luna will use perfume you hate?"

Conner chuckled as the sides of my mouth rose minutely. "What about the animal? Pebble, do you hate cats? Or whatever animal that is?"

"No, I actually didn't hunt for the first several years I was a wolf because I didn't want to hurt the animals."

"Oh."

Hollis shrugged. "I think it's just interesting that even in the premonition Luna is fighting with you instead of helping." Her tone was snide ... also not helpful.

With a sigh, I rubbed my face, trying to figure out how to mix oil and water. The tension in the room made all my muscles tight as a bowstring.

Before I could respond, Conner turned from the stove and said, "Well, I, for one, am hungry. I have enough food for everyone. People can eat together or separate, but either way, we should all eat." He faced Hollis. "And as for tomorrow, no reason to be afraid. Pebble has been turning into a wolf her entire life. She has more control than anyone I know. You'll fall in love with her furry side."

Chapter 18 – Transformation

Saturday morning, I woke up and headed to the gym. I need to work off some of my pent-up emotions. Between school, Hollis, Luna, pack, and well, everything, I had too much knocking around in my head.

After a half-hour run, I decided to do some weight lifting. I wasn't home that often, so any workout had to be full body. I had just started when Luna came into the barn. Every muscle in me tensed. There was no way I could focus with her nearby. I knew, deep in the depths of my soul, she had every right to what she felt. She wasn't obligated to stay and help me run the pack. Despite what my mind knew, in my heart, it still felt like a betrayal.

With the reliability of a server asking you how your meal is just after taking a bite, my eyes started to water. The connection of my emotion and tears was frustrating. Shutting my eyes, I tried to center myself before putting the weights away. There was no way I would be effective like this.

"Oh, are you done?" Behind me, I could hear her stretching.

"Yep. Off to shower." It took everything in me to keep my voice neutral. I tried to slip past her. Gods knew the gym was big enough, but somehow I missed my escape, and Luna reached out to grab my arm.

"Hey, hold up a minute, will ya?"

There was a chill in the air, and I wanted to yank away from her, cross my arms over my chest, and storm off, but I knew that wouldn't help. Instead, I shut my eyes. "What?" I sounded defeated.

"Are you that upset about last night?"

"No."

She choked out a laugh. "Do you want to try that again?"

"I don't know what you want me to say."

"The truth. We don't have the others here. It's just you and me, the alphas of this pack. We've never spoken about the pack's future ... our future. You've never told me what *you* want."

My muscles tensed, and I could feel the tremors starting. This couldn't be happening. "What do you want me to say, Luna?"

"Again, Pebble, I want the truth." She'd moved closer, her voice barely a whisper. "I can't make a decision about my future before I know what you, the true alpha of this pack, want. You are more than the leader here. You are family. Everyone loves and respects you. I'm not going to charge in here and make unilateral decisions without talking with you first."

I was gobsmacked. Never in a million years had I expected anything like this. "Why didn't you ask last night?"

She stepped around me until we were face to face. She rubbed my cheek, and I realized, despite my efforts, a tear had escaped my control. "I didn't want to put you on the spot," Luna said gently. "I didn't know if you wanted to face your feelings in front of so many people. Easier to have them all yell at me."

It had all been to protect me. Something in me shifted. Her stormy blue eyes seemed to penetrate through everything I felt and thought. Slowly, I lifted my hands and placed them on her hips. "I don't want people to hate you or not understand you."

She smiled, and it lit up her face. "It doesn't really matter. It's happened my whole life. The people who really matter figure it out in the end. That's all that I care about."

My lips were dry. I tried to lick them, but my mouth was dry as well. "Luna ... I want you to stay ... here. I think we make a good team. We balance each other out. I—" Closing my eyes, I bit my lip. I didn't know how to say what I needed to say. How could I tell her that I wanted to be alphas with her. Together.

I felt her mouth on mine, and everything changed.

After my shower, I dressed in jeans and a sweatshirt. Looking in the mirror, I tried to decide if I looked different—happier? Lighter? More relaxed? *Did all of that really happen?* I smiled at my reflection like I had a juicy secret.

In the kitchen, the coffee was made and the scent filled me before I even got to the mugs.

The others weren't around so I heated up a bagel and sat at the table in relative peace. A few minutes seemed like heaven.

Once I'd finished my bagel, I got up to refill my coffee and grab a banana. Hollis came into the kitchen. "Morning, Pebble. Is there anything to eat at this resort?"

I smiled wide. "I had a bagel and can make one for you. There are cereals, eggs, bacon—" I swiveled to search the closed cupboards doors, then shrugged. "I don't know, lots of things. What are you hungry for?"

"Pancakes." She smiled deviously.

Chuckling, I shook my head. "Only if you can convince one of the others." There was a commotion coming from the stairs. "Speaking of ..."

Dayna and Luna walked in. Luna's hair was still damp from her shower. Dayna narrowed her eyes at me, and I realized I was blushing.

In a rush, I opened the refrigerator door. Dayna's voice followed me. "What were you two talking about?"

Bending, I checked the bottom shelf for ... I had no idea, I just didn't feel like facing anyone. I saw a box of cold brew coffee and thought, what the heck, and grabbed one. "Hollis wants pancakes, but I'm not about to make that."

As soon as I stepped away from the refrigerator, I opened the can, as if that was exactly what I'd been after. The super sweet coffee was a bit cloying, but very caffeinated.

Conner walked in. "I can make the pancakes if you want to head out and do the wolf thing. They should be done by the time you're back." He turned to Dayna. "And maybe you could show off as well. If Hollis is going to spend any time here, maybe she should see the full menagerie?"

A huge grin lit up Dayna's face. "Oh! That sounds fun, and she'd love to come out and play. Actually, that's a really good idea. It's been a hot minute, and she's grumpy. We never talked about this, did we? I mean, I talked to Jade a bit about hands and paws, but I should practice."

Even though Dayna was connected to Luna, I could discern her stress. I placed my hand on her shoulder. "Relax. Yes, this may take a while for you to figure out, but it'll be the wolf that will probably be hard, not—"

"Oh!" she said, cutting me off. "Right, because I've had her for so long. She'll be my go-to gal."

"What are you two talking about?" Hollis snapped. "You're not making any sense." The nutmeg scent of her irritation filled the room.

Conner lifted his eyebrow. "You know, nutmeg would taste good in pancakes."

I was split between wanting to punch him and laughing.

Dayna tilted her head, then nodded. "Right. You wouldn't know without my telling you. I'm sorry. My family comes from a line of werebears. Before Pebble changed me, I already had an animal."

Eyes wide, Hollis's head snapped to Luna. "Are you a bear, too?"

"No, and stop being so dramatic."

I sighed. "Can all the people who are important to me please get along?"

The heat and frustration Hollis was throwing around was suddenly aimed at me. "Luna is one of *your* people now? Yesterday, she couldn't even commit to," her hands flew out to the sides, "whatever you were discussing. Alpha politics? Now you're claiming her as yours?"

With a strength of will, I tamped down any quick retort that leapt to mind. I reached out to clasp Hollis's upper arms and stared at her in her eyes. Deep down, I knew her anger came from a place of love and protection. She had spent her life being the barrier between me and those who were confused by this odd creature thrust into their schools. She didn't understand that here and now I wasn't in any danger.

I rubbed her arms, trying to reassure her. "Hollis, this morning Luna and I spoke. She didn't want to come to any decision without knowing where my heart lay in the matter. This is my world, and before she, you know, stepped on my toes, she wanted us to talk. We're good, okay?"

The muscles under my hands relaxed and she nodded. "Yeah. I'm just ... are you sure? Blink twice if you need me to get us alone for a longer talk."

"Can I be okay and blink twice anyway? Talking with you is just my happy place."

We laughed, then everyone but Conner headed to the back yard. At some point Fern had joined the group. They stood next to Hollis, explaining everything that happened.

"What are they doing? It's freezing out here!" Hollis all but screeched.

Off to the side, I could just hear Luna's soft chuckle.

Fern spoke softly. "They're about to shift. Their clothes at best will get in the way. At worst, they will get destroyed."

The comment about the cold was legit. There was new snow on the ground and a fierce wind that cut through clothes ... without clothes, I shut my eyes and thought, *it's time, wolf.* I really needed my fur on.

Like cracking open a cocoon, my wolf's body, fur, and soul flowed over me. My humanity got tucked away and though it hurt, it also felt natural. Once my wolf's body was in control, we trotted over to Hollis, sat, and smiled, tongue lolling out. We didn't want to scare her.

The sweet scent of fear wafted from her in waves, but we locked our muscles and didn't move. We had enough control to ignore our basic instincts.

We waited ... I waited.

Hollis's breathing hitched as she gaped at me, then shot a terrified glance at Dayna. "But Fern, she's really a bear. Like ... big and brown and real."

Fern's hand massaged Hollis's back. "You need to relax. It's just Dayna and this is just Pebble. You can pet them, but you need to calm down first."

There was a moment I thought she'd bolt, but then Hollis nodded, shut her eyes, and took a long, steadying breath. After that, she squatted in front of me, petting my head. "Okay, it's like you're a really big dog. This isn't so bad."

The longer she sat by me, the calmer she got. "God, I've always wanted a dog." She lightly swatted my nose. "You could've been like this our whole friendship, couldn't you? Then I could have had a dog all these years. You totally denied me this, Pebble."

After the swat, a tension built in the air, but her words caused both Luna and Fern to laugh.

Finally, Hollis moved over to Dayna. It took her a few more minutes, but she relaxed. "You're so beautiful. Who knew I'd ever be able to pet a bear? This is fantastic! Like, seriously amazing."

"Okay," Luna said, standing to move over to us. "I think we should let these two move around and stretch their muscles, then they'll need those pancakes."

Crunchy snow was fun when running as a wolf. Dayna and I tried to be stealthy, but our trek scared the few birds from the trees and the other animals well before we got to them. We ended up at the lake, which was fully frozen over from the cold spell. We crushed the ice and chewed some of the chunks, then headed back.

Once we shifted and dressed, we got inside to the smells of warm nutmeg pancakes, candied bacon, and eggs.

The day kept on getting better and better.

Chapter 19 – Singing To Mondara

"La tarea es muy importante para tu aprendizaje." Across from me, Hollis sat with one eyebrow raised.

The table in front of me looked like my bag had vomited papers all over it. With a bit of desperation, I flipped through some pages in my notebook. "Um ... tarea? Is that one of the verbs I'm learning to conjugate?"

"Do you ever study any of this without me?"

I blew out a breath and slumped. "I do, I promise. I just have a lot on my mind this week."

"Like what? I used to know everything ... or thought I did. Now I feel less in the know, even though I *know* more."

We sat in the main lobby on the dorm's floor, across from the elevators. It was open to anyone who could get into the building, though it was meant for students residing on our floor. When I'd made my schedule, Hollis had agreed to spend an hour or so every Monday afternoon helping me with Spanish. The problem was, I wasn't giving the subject the time and respect it deserved.

A quick sniff confirmed we were still the only two in the room. "The full moon is Wednesday. It's only my second as alpha. During the last, I was focused a lot on the new wolves, I forgot to fret over leading a pack."

A soft smile spread on Hollis's face, and she rubbed the back of my hand. "Tell me about it."

"Gods, where do I even start?"

"How about there? You've never told me the real reason you say 'gods,' have you?"

I laughed. If nothing else, Hollis was clever. "The wolves believe in twin gods, Mondara and Sonnara. One each for the sun and moon. Though they both watch over the animal and human sides of our nature, Sonnara is considered to stand more for the human side, helping us to remember our origin. Mondara watches over all the animals of the forest. They protect the run and the hunt and help us not to be detected. Have you ever thought about the fact that we're still such an unknown? We attribute that to Mondara. It's why we give in to the wolf and honor the night, singing our praises and our acceptance to our dual natures under the full moon."

Hollis's brow furrowed. "Do you have a choice?"

"No, not wolves. The other animals can decide to run other times, but wolves have a need to run on the night of the full moon."

"How many other wereanimals are there?"

"Well, you know about Dayna's bear. Jade can shift into a panther." Hollis's mouth dropped open. "Maybe the next time you see her you can ask her to shift. It's beautiful, black and sleek. She once told me she and Owen saw a weremoose. Beyond that, I have no idea about weres." I was holding back information, but she specifically asked about wereanimals.

Her eyes narrowed. "No idea about weres. Are there other things that go bump in the night? Vampires? Witches?"

"Why does everyone always immediately go to vampires? No, no undead ... at least not as far as I know. Also, I don't think there are witches. But, yeah, there are other shifter animals that aren't wereanimals."

"What's the difference?" Her scent was a combination of cinnamon annoyance and vanilla interest.

"A shifter can keep their clothes on ... apparently." I could hear the frustration in my voice and knew if there were another werecreature in the room the scent of cinnamon would overwhelm any scent of vanilla.

Before Hollis could ask anything else, Fern walked in. "How goes Spanish?"

Hollis huffed, and I laughed. Winking at Hollis, I said, "It somehow turned into a lesson on Mondara and Sonnara. Though, with my quiz coming up on Wednesday, I probably should study conjugation. I do not want to fail this class and have to retake it." I shivered.

Fern leaned over to give Hollis a kiss, and my mind immediately conjured up an image of Luna. Shaking my head, I looked down at my notes.

Spanish, I had to focus on Spanish.

Hollis asked if she could join us Wednesday night. She wanted to meet more of the pack and try to help out. After meeting my wolf and Dayna's bear, she didn't feel as nervous. Now that this part of my life was open to her, she felt like she wanted to be all in. She also promised not to snap at Luna.

When we walked into pack house, Easton and Tanner were in the kitchen cooking. The house smelled like seasoning, home, and heaven. My belly did a small cheer, and I had to agree with it.

"Wow, that smells amazing. How often do you have other people cook for you?"

Laughter echoed from the kitchen. A light feminine sound. Monica, Tanner's wife and a former teacher of both me and Hollis, poked her head around the corner. "Pebble, you're here early." Her eyes landed on Hollis. "Oh! Ms. Panto, it's been a few years. I hear you're Pebble's roommate. Kudos on making it to college."

Hollis froze. Then she shook her head. "Mrs. Billings? What are you doing here?"

Monica reached out and slid her hand down Hollis's arm. "I know this is hard. So many changes in your life and they are coming at you at top speed."

Hollis's head shook in denial. "But ... are you a werewolf too? Is everyone a werewolf? Have I been surrounded my whole life?"

A small chuckle escaped our former teacher. "No, dear. I'm like you, just a person. No extra animal soul riding within me. My husband is Tanner. I believe you've met him. And my son, Easton, you may have seen him as well. They were both there when you were attacked. They help Pebble solve problems."

Both Hollis's shoulders dropped, and her jaw relaxed. "Okay, good. I get it. So it's really okay for people to be here who don't have," her hands shimmied up and down her in front of her body, "animals?"

Warmth emanated from Monica. "Yes, of course. That's why Pebble brought you. It's always helpful to have people here to watch over the kids. Right now there's only one, but in a few years there will be more, I'm sure. It always goes in waves. And then there's cleaning up after dinner and setting up for breakfast, especially on a weekday full moon."

"Mom! You're cooking in here!" Easton yelled. "Or have you forgotten?"

"First off, you are more than capable of finishing what I was working on, and second, do you need to bellow? We're only a few feet away. Really, Easton, you're not a kid anymore." She'd spoken no louder than when she'd started talking to us. She knew how well werewolves could hear, especially when they were trying.

I laughed, hooked my arm in Hollis's, and led her into the house. "Okay, Easton. I'll stop distracting your mom. I realize everything will burn and fail if she's not there to supervise." From the kitchen, I heard Tanner snort. "Fern, Hollis, and I will just be in the living room, taking in all the smells. Unless you want *me* to help."

There was a growl from the kitchen, but I doubted any of the others with me could hear it. Tanner's low voice sounded amused. "I would rather not have to start over. You may not be as bad as Jade, but the three of us are doing fine without you, boss."

As Monica returned to the kitchen, I slowly took a sniff of the air. Piper, Julez, and their child Spruce were here, as were Piper's parents.

It was early, and I assumed most of the pack were still at work.

Over the next couple hours, the rest of the wolves in human form arrived, including Luna, Dayna, and Conner. As people came that Hollis didn't know, I introduced them. For some, I gave a bit of a background, letting both

Hollis and the pack member know more about each other.

Many of the individuals, like Aunt Allison, Andy, and Fred and Janet, Bevin's parents, family who spent a lot of time with me as I grew up, had heard stories about Hollis, and finally getting to meet her was nice for them.

After dinner, Chloe collected Hollis and Fern to head to the basement to play games with Spruce.

Within me, I felt the connections to all the wolves become tighter, clearer. If I shut my eyes, I could pinpoint where each person was in and outside of the house. Who had shifted and who was finishing up last minute chores.

Luna came up and slid her arm around my waist. "Is it just me, or can you ... I don't know, *feel* everyone more?"

"I can, and there's almost a glow, like the aura surrounding them is merging, getting brighter. I may have to ask your mom about that." I hoped my voice didn't sound whiny.

Luna laughed. "Do you want me there? I can maybe help run interference. I know she can be a lot at times."

I liked how our arms fit so naturally around each other, and I playfully squeezed her. "That seems to run in the family."

"Well, maybe." There was a pause, then Luna looked out at the back yard where Andy and Chris started their shift to wolves. "Do you think this intensity is just for the moon, or will our awareness of everyone continue to grow?"

Piper and Julez were done in the basement and about to head up to do their own transformation. A tremor ran down my body at the idea that this would be the new normal. "I think this is a full moon thing, to help us keep track of everyone. If it were an always thing, Mom or Dad or even one of the California alphas, you know, Jade's pack, they would've told me."

"Okay, good." She leaned into me. "Ready to go find fur?"

My smile made me feel lighter and on instinct I leaned in to kiss her cheek. It was the first time I'd done it, and it made me feel giddy. "I am."

We separated and headed to the back yard. It wouldn't take me long to find my wolf, so I let Luna go first. This would be her third time with paws under her, and I wanted to make sure she could do it. Dayna came out, and I walked her through her shift as well.

"Think of your paw ... not a bear's paw but a wolf's smaller paw with her sharp claws."

Dayna bit her lip and gazed at me a bit nervously. "I don't want to run as a bear. Could you call my wolf and let me try this another time?"

Part of me wanted to see what would happen if she tried on her own, but if she failed, she'd be unhappy. Kneeling, I gazed into her dark brown eyes. The presence of the bear was frustrated with my invasion, but I let a bit of the mantle out and the bear backed off. Her wolf perked up. *That's it, beautiful one. Now, come out and join us.* "Dayna, shift." I put power behind my words.

It took a few more seconds, but her transformation finally began.

When I turned, I saw Luna morphing. It was slow and looked painful. New wereanimals always had that problem. I decided to wait until she had her head back in place and knew who she was, in case she attacked, before I found my wolf. A wild alpha didn't sound like a great idea.

True to form, once she was wolf, she lunged. I caught her, letting all of my mantle out. Around us, a few wolves whined. I heard them as they dropped to the snow.

She finally relented, though her snarl didn't abate until my power was put away.

Finally, it was my turn. On my hands and knees, I told my wolf it was time, and she was happy to come out and play. She loved how much paw time she'd had over the last few weeks.

We led the pack through the woods. The weather was warmer tonight, though I didn't think that would last. We stretched our legs. The aroma of cold snow, pine trees, and squirrels were on the air.

Luna caught a scent and signaled she wanted to lead. Everyone followed.

I felt a heat in my chest, my wolf warning me to back away. After a moment, I realized she followed a skunk's trail. Groaning, I tried to alter her direction, but it was too late. She got a snout full of punishment for her trouble.

Shocked, but more angry than upset, Luna didn't let a bit of spray stop her from her quarry. I could almost hear her thinking, 'I already stink, may as well get dinner for my trouble.'

Amusement ran through the pack as she stalked her prey and took it down. After that, everyone gave her a wide berth.

As we continued our run, I tried knocking on Conner's mental door.

"Oh ... hi. Pebble?"

"Hi, Conner. I don't know how competent you feel in using this ability, but can you reach people back home? Like Helen or Fern?"

There was a pause and I wondered if the connection was lost. Tanner signaled he'd found something, and the group followed him.

"Yes, I can reach Fern. What should I say to them?"

Relief flooded me. It amused me that the epsilon and soon to be epsilon could connect, though I wasn't too surprised. These wolves were always coming up with new things they could do. *"Can you ask them to look up getting the skunk smell out of a dog and have that ready for when we get back? I want to be prepared."*

A wash of understanding and amusement flooded me from his direction. *"Can do."*

Tanner caught a rabbit, as did Andy. It wasn't a huge hunting night, but the pack seemed satisfied. We ran to the lake for chunks of ice, then headed home. Being a school and work night, no one would complain about a shorter run.

Back home Hollis and Fern waited with a bucket, the hose, and towels.

Chapter 20 – A Change Of Heart

Thursday morning, I found a shirt Owen had given me for my previous birthday. Slipping it on, I headed to the kitchen to eat as everyone ran through to head to work.

Luna came down after her shower and scowled at my shirt. Then she chuckled. *"I believe in you, but I also believe in werewolves, so don't get too excited. That's kind of funny."*

I shimmied my shoulders and smiled. "My brother got it for me. It makes me laugh."

The others finally joined us, having gotten themselves ready for the day. Like me, Fern had decided on snark. Their shirt said: *Were They.*

At this, Luna shook her head. "Shouldn't you have worn that yesterday, or does that mean you're only nonbinary on the days of the full moon?"

Fern looked down at their shirt. "No, it means my soul is nonbinary, and I can bring it out when I want, but it *has* to come out with the full moon."

"That makes sense." Hollis wrapped her arms around Fern's waist. "But do you bite and have fangs?"

Fern practically purred. "I thought we figured that out already."

Hollis blushed.

Tanner drove us all back to campus. There were six of us who needed to get to class, and logistically it was easier than calling multiple cabs. March's full moon was on a Friday, respectable, but April's wouldn't be. May's, like during fall semester, was during finals week, so that would be all sorts of fun. I decided to put transportation on my list of worries for each full moon with pack members in college.

Once the day began, classes ate up my time, and then homework finished it up. I wanted to be done with the lion's share of school work before the weekend.

Besides Spanish words to memorize, I had two papers to write. Laser focused on getting everything done, I nearly jumped when the lights in the room flashed on and off. "Pebble. It's after midnight, you have to stop working."

My body creaked as I straightened and turned to gape at Hollis. "What now?" Squinting, I looked at my phone to confirm what she'd said.

She came over and squeezed my shoulders. "You have to give a tour tomorrow. Get some sleep or you'll end up walking everyone into the lake."

"Well, it's still frozen, so only *onto* the lake." I winked at her as I put my books away. "I think I finally have everything memorized for next week's Spanish class. When the professora talks, I can spend the time learning the lesson, not trying to translate."

"About time," Hollis said, shaking her head. "You are so smart ... until you're not. But that doesn't diminish the fact that you need to stop studying for a bit. You're overloading yourself."

I leaned my head back and it landed on her chest. "Yes, Mom." My eyes drifted closed, and I realized after the run the night before and a full day of classes and studying, I really was tired. "Okay, you're right. Bed."

With a bit of effort, I managed to stand. After a quick visit to the bathroom, I collapsed into bed and may have fallen asleep on the way down.

My dream started off with me floating over endless flowers. Two horses ran across the field and the flowers took flight. I realized they were butterflies, not plants. Then three crows dove down across the path of the horses. Their loud caws woke me up.

I sat up and rubbed my eyes. The sun slanted in through the window, low on the horizon, but bright enough to tell me I may as well stay up. Despite the dream, it felt like I'd just blinked, and the night had flown by.

Hollis still slept, so, as quietly as I could, I gathered clothes and headed to the shower. It was early and no one else was in the bathroom. Having the room to myself was a dorm luxury. The heat seeped into me and convinced me to stay awake.

Once dressed, I headed back to the room and put the final touches on the paper I'd been writing the night before. Before Hollis interrupted me, I'd been struggling with how to word my thoughts. She'd been right. It only took about twenty minutes and the paper was done. I snarled at the silly paper and how much stress it'd given me.

Not wanting to wake up Hollis with the coffee press, or face the dorm's coffee, or food, I decided to head to Electric Brew to get something better. In reality, I took any excuse to head to my favorite spot.

The coffee shop was in the wrong direction from my classes, but not by far. When I got to the café, the line was long so when it was my turn, I ordered two breakfast sandwiches, a cappuccino, and a large coffee to go.

I took my goods and found a spot at the bar by the window. The cappuccino and first sandwich went down, soothing my soul. *I wonder if it would be reasonable to get a fancy espresso machine for the pack den. Waking up to lattes or cappuccinos would be amazing.*

The fantasy amused me. I debated making a memo to add the question to the next pack meeting. Or maybe we could add a poll to the pack website, now that we had one.

After clearing my first coffee mug and food wrappers, I headed towards the tour meeting place with the second coffee. It wasn't as decadent as the first, but it was big, full of caffeine, and I needed all the fortification I could get for the day.

There was a cool breeze, and I worried about how many people would actually be on the tour. It seemed people canceled on these colder days. I hugged my clipboard to my chest, waiting for all of the people to find me.

Some tour days, I looked over the names of everyone who'd registered. Others, like today, I didn't bother. In the beginning, I had some weird notion of learning the names of the clients who signed up so I could talk to them more informally. It didn't take many outings to realize both that I was horrible at names, and that it would be impossible for me to memorize that many people so quickly. If I wanted to be personal, they all wore nametags.

Over the next thirty minutes, people trickled in, and I checked them off. When half the people had checked in,

I finally decided to scan the other names. That's when I saw it: Hollis. Hollis had signed up for today's tour.

Grumbling, I plastered on a smile and got everyone else situated. My roommate was one of the last to show up. As she sauntered to the group, I narrowed my eyes at her. She smiled wide. "What?"

"That's what I want to know. You know this campus. Why the tour?"

One of her shoulders bobbed. "I'll explain as we walk."

It took all my strength not to shake her. With my smile forcibly in place, I turned to the rest of the group and began my job.

The clients had a lot of questions. Some were obvious, and I had to take a beat to make sure my answers didn't sound snarky.

"Since this is the cheese state, do they give every student free cheese when they apply?" The boy snorted after he asked his question.

"No, but down State Street there are some amazing stores where you can buy local cheeses, including restaurants with fantastic fried cheese curds." My smile became real thinking about my favorite treat.

His father patted his back. "How many students are admitted?"

"Last year, there were just over sixty thousand applicants. Just under twenty-eight thousand students were admitted, though under eight thousand actually ended up coming here. The University is competitive and has an almost ninety percent graduation rate."

When we got to the end of the tour, I gave my final words and sent everyone on their way.

Hollis came up to me. "I was hoping we could talk. I wanted some time without anyone else. I feel like we're always with others."

"Sure. And you know we can always take a walk and get away from the others, just you and me. You're my best friend and I'll always have time for you."

Her body relaxed as a smile spread on her face. "Yeah, I know. I just ... it's hard."

"Did you want to talk about school? The dorms? Or was it ... you know, doggos?"

"That last one. I've been thinking about it ... you know, a lot. You're my best friend, you always have been. And I really like Fern. I don't know what it is, but from the moment I met them, it just feels right. Watching you change last weekend, it was really—" She stopped talking and looked across the mall, gazing at some people huddled in their coats, walking towards the library.

The wind was blowing in the wrong direction, and I didn't know what she wanted to say. I hoped it wasn't that she still feared wolves and hated the idea of the world I came from, but paranoia at losing her struck deep. My wolf tried to sooth me, but Hollis was just too important.

"I can't help you with this, Hollis. I need you to say the words. Tell me what you're thinking." I tried not to let the stress show. Nothing in my mind or soul could've prepared me for having any conversation about werewolves with my best friend.

She licked her lips, then turned and clasped my hands. "Pebble, I've had time to really think about everything. I've thought about it all. I want ... I want to join you."

A numb chill ran down my spine. Despite this being a deep dark secret dream of mine, I couldn't just leap up and yell, 'Yes!' This was serious ... I had to be the alpha. "You understand that not only is this a lifelong thing, it will probably include Luna."

Her jaw clenched and the muscles in her upper body tensed as if I'd slapped her. Then she breathed slowly. "If you think that's the best choice for you, then yes, I can accept her, too."

I squeezed her hands. "As much as I may want to, this isn't something either of us should rush into. Let me arrange a meeting with some people next weekend. That will give us both time to think about this and if you're still set on it, then we can make sure all the correct steps are taken."

Hollis bit her lower lip. "There are correct steps?"

Pulling her into a tight hug, I nodded. "There are when I have time to take them."

Chapter 21 – A Touch Of Training

It took me most of a week to get my ducks in a row. On Wednesday I sent an email out asking Aunt Allison, Tanner, and Piper's mom, Helen, to meet with me and Hollis the following Saturday.

On Thursday, in our Folklore class, we had assigned seats based on groups. I had been put in a group with Dayna. I asked her about her plans, and she said she'd be there Saturday. That left Conner and Luna.

Luna was also in the class and the lecture was a bit boring. I leaned back and thought about the weekend. If I were to boil it down to three thoughts it would be the pack house, Hollis, and teaching ... a person at a blackboard. With a bit of concentration, I formed the images in my mind, preparing to send them to Luna.

Will Luna understand? I could do more, but I don't want to distract too much from her taking notes.

Well, there's only one way to find out.

The professor's voice became white noise as I focused on Luna, the images I wanted her to get from me, and sending them to her. After I gave a *push* of—something—I felt a bit drained. I needed to make sure I ate more, and maybe brought food with me, like I told Conner to do.

To my right, I saw Luna shake her head. Then she whipped around and pinned me with a piercing stare.

She gazed at me for a few seconds as if she were trying to read my mind. Then, if possible, her eyes narrowed more. An image of Hollis flashed in my head, then a gray wolf, then Hollis again, finally a school building. When the images were done, Luna turned back to her notebook.

I was about to return to my notes when the image of me falling back from Luna as a goose popped into my head, along with the sound of a scream. The sound was in Luna's voice, since I hadn't actually screamed.

'Why?'

'Because you could've just asked if I was up to helping teach Hollis instead of the cryptic images.'

'We're in class, I didn't want to distract you.'

There was a harrumph and then it all went silent.

I wanted to groan or laugh at what we'd done. Then Luna shook her head and turned to me again, the stormy focus of her gaze on me as she smirked. One last image burned its way across my mind. An intimate round table with a tablecloth. A candle in the center. And two chairs.

When I could concentrate on my surroundings again, Luna eyed me with one eyebrow raised, a question on her face. *Is she asking me on a date?*

My heart pounded hard in my chest. The last time this had happened, it was to learn our abilities, not a real date. This seemed like more. *Am I really ready?* Another image popped up in my head of me kissing her cheek. Swallowing, I slowly nodded letting the giddy smile I felt show.

Once class was over, everyone started to pack up and leave. I moved slowly, letting everyone leave ahead of me. Luna came up and smirked. "So, are we going out tonight or tomorrow night?"

My nerves tried to paralyze my muscles, but I squeezed my hands together. This was Luna after all. "Probably tonight." I forced myself to move, gathering my stuff and standing as I spoke. "Everyone will be heading to the pack house tomorrow and I should be there for Hollis. But tonight there are no requirements on my time."

The side of Luna's mouth twitched. "So, you'll only be focused on me and our date?"

Part of me wondered when I'd lost control of the conversation. Another part wondered if I'd ever had it. "Something like that."

"Good. I'll meet you out front of your dorm at seven." She spun and sauntered away.

My mind went blank for a moment, then I slowly followed.

In the hall, Fern and Hollis waited for me. Hollis stared in the direction Luna went, but Fern looked at me. "You okay?"

"Yep, I'm dandy. You?"

"Absolutely. Classes are done for the week. We can go, study, and relax for the rest of the evening." Fern smiled. "Unless there's something else you have planned for tonight?"

My head tilted and I looked at them skeptically. "Did you hear our conversation?"

"We weren't eavesdropping, if that's what you're asking." Hollis said, turning to face me. "But you weren't talking that softly." She snorted. "You have a date with Luna?" I could tell she tried not to sound scandalized, which was a step in the right direction, especially if she really did want to join the pack.

"I guess."

She reached out and clasped my lower arm. "Is that a good thing?"

Clenching my jaw, I forced a smile. "I think so. If she's going to stay and be alpha with me ... because I asked her to, she and I need to really get to know each other. Don't you think?"

Hollis slumped. "You're right. Well, if you're going on a date with her, we should spend the next few hours getting you ready."

That made me laugh. No one could switch their attitude on dating so fast. Shaking my head, I followed her back to the dorms. I knew I had a few outfits that would work back home, but I hadn't brought them to the dorms. I could do my own make-up, but if I was honest, Hollis was much better at applying the stuff than I was.

In the end I wore a dark green cocktail dress that Hollis had tucked in the back of her closet and black ballet sandals. My short hair meant there wasn't much I *could* do with it ... thankfully. Hollis lent me a small black purse and a stylish black coat she'd picked up from a second-hand store. When I checked out my reflection, I was impressed.

By five to seven, I was just inside the doors. It was too cold to wait outside. Luna was also early, and coming in, she demanded to see what I'd decided to wear. "Once again, you clean up well, alpha. I'm impressed."

Smirking, I decided I was done playing games. Leaning over, I kissed her cheek. "Thanks. It's what I live for."

She laughed, then we walked to State Street and found a nice Italian restaurant. After a couple of minutes of searching the menu, we each ordered.

"Do you want me to join the pack because of what your wolf showed you or because of me?"

When we'd been seated, the server had brought free breadsticks. I had been about to take a bite of one, but that stopped me cold. "What?"

"You heard me. Before I make my final decision, Pebble, I want to know your reasoning for asking me to stay. Is it me or your wolf? Is it us or the pack?"

My mouth opened and closed a few times, and I figured I looked like a fish out of water. Finally, I sighed. "I don't know how to do this, Luna. I don't even know what I'm feeling."

"Are you feeling hate or revulsion? I mean, you've shown some affection and there was that one kiss, but I'd like to know what you're actually thinking. Words."

My face heated so fast, I thought my head would explode. "Okay, right. You deserve that." I closed my eyes for a moment to try and sort my thoughts. After taking a slow breath, I sipped my water. I braced myself and stared Luna in the eyes, knowing I had to be honest. My hands shook, so I placed them on the table and tried to relax. "Luna, I want you to stay because of you. I think we work well together and *are* good together. If you don't think the 'we' is or should be part of the equations, I get it, but—" I stopped to breathe. "Gods above, this is hard."

She leaned over and placed a soft kiss on my lips. "If you're willing to give this a solid girl scout try, then so am I. I just needed to hear that you were all in as well."

My lips tingled and I smiled. "I am. All of this." I waved my hand at us and the table. "I really don't know what I'm doing, but I want to try with you and—" My breath was shaky, but I wanted her to hear this. "Why is this so difficult?."

"You don't have to say more, you know that, right?" She reached over and placed her hand over mine.

"I know, I just ..." I slumped. "We've sort of talked about this before. I've never done this. I've never even wanted to do it. It's kind of terrifying."

Luna chuckled. "You went after lone wolves without batting an eye. You lead a pack at eighteen. You're like a superhero. But dating me? That's where you draw the line of scary?"

Hearing how she described me, I felt strong and desirable. On instinct, I leaned over to kiss her. My heart beat faster than any run I'd even done as a wolf and when I sat back I felt both empowered and panicked. "It's not you I'm afraid of dating, Luna. It's these feelings of wanting to date anyone that have my mind whirling. I honestly never really thought it would ever happen to me."

She stroked my wrist and smiled. "Well, Pebble Stone, let's see if we can take over the world together."

We spent the rest of the meal talking about our classes and a bit about Luna's upbringing.

On the walk home, Luna slid her arm around me. "Listen, I don't want to push you into anything you're not comfortable doing. You're going to have to lead."

I found her far hip with my hand and pulled her in a bit closer to me as we finished the walk to the dorms. "Thank you. You don't know how much those words mean to me."

On Saturday morning, after my trip to the gym, I met Conner in the kitchen where he was up early making French toast, bacon, and eggs. I found some fruit in the fridge and started making something lighter to go with breakfast.

By nine, everyone was up and those I'd invited had arrived. We all sat in the dining room where there were enough seats we could all eat together. Once everyone had their first round of coffee, I leaned back. "As some of you know, Hollis has requested to become part of the pack."

Tanner narrowed his eyes. "I thought you didn't want to become a wolf?"

Hollis sat up straighter. "I know, but at the time I was scared. I've spent more time around all of you and now know more than I did. I believe my life will be spent here and because of that, I'd like to be fully part of the pack."

Helen regarded her. "You do know you can be fully part of the pack without growing claws and howling to the moon once a month, right? I don't feel any less welcome for not being a wolf."

I let her words penetrate for a moment as everyone thought about that. Then I reached over and rubbed Hollis's arm. "Today isn't about trying to convince you to not join the pack. It also isn't about convincing you to become a wolf. What I want to do is set up a schedule where you spend the next two weeks learning about what it means to be a pack werewolf. I know you'd prefer if it was just me, but in reality, getting different perspectives is a better way to learn. Tanner has been the right hand to the alpha for as long as I can remember. If he brings Easton on his training day for Hollis, he'll have the person who'll probably fill his shoes one day. Aunt Allison is a submissive wolf, she's all the way at the other end of the spectrum. Then we have Helen who didn't learn about werewolves until years after marrying one. Dayna, Luna, and Conner can tell you about their experience both as new wolves and as being newly shifted at college. It's not easy. And Conner can tell you what it was like being brought up in a different pack. Each person has something they can teach you."

"Even Fern?" Hollis asked, a smile playing across her face.

"Yes," I said with some certainty. "They were trained in a different pack, like Conner. They'll bring in their own perspective. Not to mention, being raised first in a pack, then as a lone wolf, Fern has a very unique way of looking at things."

Once my plan was laid out, everyone got their calendars and started setting up a schedule. The next full moon would be in three weeks. If everything went as planned, I would bite Hollis in two. We had two weeks to ensure that Hollis knew what she was getting into and wouldn't revert to being afraid, wouldn't hate me for biting her, wouldn't regret this decision.

After the planning meeting, I pulled Hollis and Fern to the side. "Okay, it's February twenty-first. I know you thought I forgot, but I didn't. What do you want to do tonight for your birthday, birthday-girl?"

Hollis blushed. "I ... ah. Well, I did think you forgot, so much else is happening. Umm, can we go out for sushi?"

I groaned and Fern smiled. "That sounds amazing."

We all headed to one of the pack cars and I took the three of us out for sushi and ice cream. It had been some time since the three of us could just be silly friends, and Hollis's birthday seemed like a great excuse.

Chapter 22 – A Decision Made Can't Be Undone

Over the next two weeks, Hollis spent as much time studying werewolf lore as she did her college classes. She took to the subject fully and every indication that I could see told me she loved what she learned.

"In every movie I've seen, werewolves are all about dominance and fighting, but you're telling me it doesn't have to be that way?" She sat crossed-legged on her bed, eyes alight. Fern perched next to her.

Dayna sat at my desk and Conner at Hollis's desk. Luna sat next to me, our shoulders touching. Though we didn't need everyone here for the lessons, it was nice to get different perspectives when we could.

This was a tricky question, and I wanted to make sure I answered it completely. "There is a hierarchy to werewolf society. At times, werewolves feel their place is wrong, and if the others in the pack disagree, there can be a fight. When there is a fight, it's usually to the death. This really hasn't happened in the Wisconsin pack in my lifetime. But this is why the Tennessee pack is in such disarray."

A dull laugh escaped Fern. "Wow. You know, there weren't really any in Tennessee before my family left, but I kept in contact with a couple of my friends, the other kids for the pack. I guess a couple of years after my family left, the muscling for position started. It apparently happened a lot. It got to the point where most of the fights stopped going to death or it would've been too much. I think the old alphas liked to watch the battles ... they encouraged them."

Sitting near the window, Conner rubbed the back of his neck. "Huh. We didn't really have any of the dominance fights in Florida. I can't remember seeing any, kind of like Pebble."

A slow smile stretched across my face. Next to me Luna eyed me. "You have a theory, don't you. You mentioned something before, and this just feeds into it, doesn't it?"

"Maybe. I wanted to talk to my parents or Jade, but I really feel like this may be a thing."

She hooked her arm around my waist and gave it a squeeze. "Just tell us already."

"Okay." I laughed. "I think having the epsilon wolves, even in human form before their first shift, calms the pack. It just makes everyone have a natural chill. The Tennessee alphas, if I were to guess, were a bit ... intense. While Fern lived with them, they toned them down, but once they left all bets were off. As for Florida and here, well, they had years with Conner and Jade in residence. My guess is, most packs don't need the influence of the epsilon, most wolves are happy as they are, but *with* the epsilon, it could take a lot to get that worried over something as trivial as rank."

Across the room, Hollis scratched her head. "Does rank mean anything?"

Before I could answer, Conner leaned forward and said, "Not really. It matters if you're alpha and the next in line, because if anything happens to the alpha, everyone will look to you to keep everyone safe. The only other ranking that matters are the submissive wolves. They are the heart of the pack."

Next to Hollis, Fern nodded. "Probably when packs were more isolated, didn't live in big cities, spent most of their time as norms, it mattered. But in today's urban world, we're just people who have another form." They looked at Dayna and Luna. "Or a couple of other forms."

The citrus scent of excitement filled the room. Hollis gazed at each of them. "So ... Saturday I'll get bitten and become a wolf."

I shook my head. "No, this weekend I'll bite you. The full moon isn't for another week."

By Saturday, Hollis buzzed with excitement. She'd had time with more than the people I'd spoken with two weeks prior. Several other pack members had been around when she'd come to pack house and helped to answer questions and guide her through what she needed to know as a new wolf.

It was nice being able to train someone before they got bitten. Having the time to really get Hollis fully acclimated prior to the bite was a novel change that I decided I could really get used to.

"Okay," I said, smiling at her. "First things first, a light breakfast."

She gaped at me. "I'm too nervous to eat. I'm about to let a wolf attack me!" Though I knew she was excited and ready, her voice quivered at those words. I wondered if she thought about being attacked in January or if that night ever gave her nightmares. Having Fern around would help.

"Right, but maybe a piece of toast to settle your belly?"

At that, Hollis took a slow breath. "Right, that's a good idea. I'm just really scattered. This is ... I can't change my mind, can I?"

Sitting next to her at the kitchen table, Fern slipped an arm around her shoulders. "Right now? Of course you can. Nothing has happened yet."

Hollis took a slow, wavering breath. "No, I mean, I really want this, but if, say, in three years I decide I don't want to turn furry once a month—" She let the statement hang.

I shrugged. "Yep, at that point there's no going back and undoing this. It's not like a tattoo, something you can easily change your mind about."

That made her snort out a laugh. Our senior year, a varsity basketball player got a tattoo of a naked lady on his arm after partying with his friends. His parents wanted him to get it removed because they didn't like it. His coach wanted it removed for propriety at a game young kids would watch. Since he hadn't been signed to a college yet, he agreed.

He was in our English class, and he complained about how hard the process was. Once it was gone, Hollis looked at him wide eyed and asked him why he didn't just wear long sleeves for the rest of the season. The look of shock and pain on his face made up for a few of the pranks he'd played on other students over the years.

After she ate her toast, she nodded, "Okay, right, more permanent than a tattoo. Got it." Her smile was painfully big. "I'm ready."

In the back yard, Aunt Allison set up a stretcher for Hollis to lie down on. It was cold, though not as bad as it had been back in January. A blanket was put under the stretcher and a second blanket over Hollis until I was ready to do my part. Hollis, to make this easier for me, only wore shorts and a halter top.

Next to her, there to support her, were Fern and Aunt Allison. Tanner, Clare, and Luna were available to stop me if for some reason I lost control. I was more worried about pushing past the revulsion of biting my best friend. *I can't believe I'm doing this.*

Though I'd done this before, Tanner knelt down and said, "Don't forget, a couple of bites on her thigh should be enough. She's a norm. But if you want to be certain, get a bite in on her belly as well. There's a bucket of water waiting to wash out your mouth when you're done, then run to move." Once he was done speaking, he scratched my neck and stood.

I eyed Aunt Allison, giving her the signal as I approached Hollis. She lifted the blanket, and I darted in to infect my best friend. *Gods above and praise Mondara, I never thought I'd be doing this.* Pushing past my hesitancy and revulsion I bit. Once, twice, and the heat of her radiated out. I chomped up a bit higher.

Hollis whimpered and I moved away quickly, rinsing my mouth out then running as fast as I could to stretch my muscles. A voice in the back of my mind questioned if biting Hollis would scare her enough that she'd be scared of me all over again. Part of me wanted to hide like the kid I wasn't anymore; another needed to return and find out how my friend fared.

The branches of the trees raked my fur, and the cool air helped release my tension. After I had run for about ten to fifteen minutes, I turned and headed back. The back yard was empty except for my clothes on the porch.

Once I shifted, Luna stood by my clothes holding a mug of hot chocolate. "You did good, alpha. Get dressed. The others are watching over Hollis."

Once I had my clothes on, she handed me the warm drink, then gave me a hug. "You don't tell anyone how hard that is."

I relaxed into the embrace. "You know?"

"I could feel it in you, in our connection. I don't think anyone else could tell, though."

I let myself sink into her, releasing some of my tension. Then, taking a breath, I pulled back. "After I'd been made a wolf, it took years for me to be able to hunt. It's still hard sometimes. I know this is what she wanted, but the idea of purposefully biting a human ... after everything that happened to me when I was a kid, it goes against my nature."

"I could help, you know."

Closing my eyes, I rested my forehead on her shoulder. "Thank you." I sighed. "Thank you for seeing me and being here. I don't know with two animals if you can, though your second isn't a wereanimal. We should test it out." I pulled back and smiled at her wickedly.

She laughed. A cold breeze reminded us we were outside, and we both turned to head inside.

Hollis was in the medical room with Aunt Allison. Fern told us she was doing well and according to Conner, she had a wolf, willing and ready to play in a week.

Chapter 23 – Family

Tanner came up and gave me a hug. "Do you want me to bake mac and cheese or order Thai for dinner?"

My stomach growled. "Gods yes. All of it!"

He laughed. "You no longer get a vote."

From the living room, Dayna said, "I haven't had Thai in a while. I vote Thai."

"Agreed," said Conner.

Luna nodded. "Isn't Thai your favorite food?"

It occurred to me she knew this about me, but I didn't know her favorite food. I just nodded, dumbfounded. She turned to Tanner. "Go with Thai. No one should have to cook tonight."

He gave her a small smile, then nodded. Taking out his phone, he started typing as he walked away.

Before we followed, I wrapped my hand around Luna's arm. "I feel like I'm behind in this dating game. How is it you know what I love to eat, and I don't know that about you?"

The side of her mouth curved up in a smirk. "You, dear Pebble, do not have a poker face. And on our very first night here, we had Thai food, because it was your favorite."

"You remember that?"

"My mom told me we were destined to be mates. I had no idea if she was right or wrong, but I'd never known her to be wrong. So, I took mental notes." She winked. "It's why I was so nice to you."

My mouth dropped open. "Nice?"

Her smirk stretched out into a full smile. "You are fun to play with. I can't foresee this becoming boring."

She started to pull away, but I held tight. Her brow rose, but I just narrowed my eyes. She knew what I wanted to know. Chuckling, she said, "If we're by the ocean, seafood. But here in Wisconsin? Brats and cheese curds. Those devils are crazy good."

Dumbfounded and amused, I threw my head back and laughed.

We headed to the living room. Luna and I sat on the couch with Dayna. Conner took a recliner. Fern sat on the love seat. I turned to them. "Fern, your parents are coming this week, right? Do you know when? Do you want to help get a room set up for them?"

"Yeah, they're planning on driving up on Wednesday. They'll probably drive home on Sunday. That way they'll have enough time to visit the pack and see the campus. Mom wants to show Dad around."

Luna bumped shoulders with me. "Maybe they'll go on your tour Friday."

My face scrunched up, and I groaned. "Sonnara save me, no. Too many of you have jumped onto my tours! But, no, I swapped tours and am doing Thursday afternoon, so I have all day Friday to be with the pack."

Aunt Allison came into the living room and sat next to Fern. We all watched her, the tension amping up with her arrival.

She reached over and squeezed Fern's wrist. "Hollis is doing great. She just passed out after she was bitten. It's not uncommon. You can go in and see for yourself; she's already healing."

Fern's face tightened and they leapt up and darted for the medical suit. I made to stand, but Aunt Allison shook her head. "Give them some time alone. Hollis should be up by dinner. You can see her then."

Tanner came in and sat next to Aunt Allison. "Easton will be here in about a half-hour with the food. Did I hear that Ronny and Amy are coming to town?"

With a grunt I stood. "Yep, and I should get a room ready for them. I have a half-hour before I go into a self-inflicted food coma."

After classes on Wednesday, several of us headed to the den to meet Fern's parents. Because Fern's parents were important to Tennessee's pack's future, I wanted Luna there so we had both alphas to welcome them. Fern wanted their parents to meet Hollis, so she joined us as well.

Since some of the pack members knew Amy from when she'd gone to college in Madison, I wasn't surprised when we walked in, and Tanner and Easton were cooking. He grumbled in his low voice, "I told the others to wait until Friday. They don't need a circus on their first night."

The four of us sat along the counter to watch the two cook. They moved so smoothly together, it was beautiful.

At the knock at the door, Fern shot up and went to answer. I swiveled, knocking shoulders with Luna to signal her we should follow.

"Mom, Dad, it's great to see you!" Fern's voice drifted to us.

"I'm just glad to be out of that car," Ronald's voice grumbled back.

Amy sighed. "I haven't been here in years. I swear, it feels like I'm coming home, even though I was only part of this pack for a few years."

Luna and I got to the hall, and I smiled at the couple. "Welcome to our den. This is Luna, the other alpha of the Wisconsin pack. And you are welcome to stay as long as you want." I shook Ronald's hand, but Amy pulled me in for a big hug.

Standing tall, Luna reached out a hand to each of Fern's parents and gave them a small smile. "Welcome to our home."

My breath hitched at her words, and I missed Fern's parents' response. Luna placed her hand on my back and a wave of images and feeling of amusement flashed through my mind, almost too fast to catch. I shook my head and shot her a glance as she gave me a small smile.

"Let them get further than the front door, kids. There's a full house and dinner's almost done." There was amusement in Tanner's voice.

A laugh bubbled out of me. "Let me show you to your room and you can clean up. Then, yes, Tanner and his son have made a fantastic dinner."

Fern shook their head. "I'll show them. It's in the basement, right?"

Amy's eyes widened. "Tanner Billings? Did you learn to cook from your parents?" She leaned in. "He and Oscar, his brother, used to compete when Oscar came to visit. It wasn't often, but those were the best weekends."

We moved to the kitchen, and Amy gave Tanner a hug. He introduced Easton. Then Fern introduced Hollis. Finally, Fern brought their parents down to where they'd be staying.

The evening went well, and the next morning Amy woke early and drove us all to campus for our classes. "I loved going to school here. I hope the four of you love it as much as I did."

Fern leaned over to hug their mom. "I'm really glad I came here, Mom. It's as great a place as you promised."

Classes seemed to drag. There was one more week before spring break, so all the professors asked us to prepare for exams and papers. I knew I'd need to study a lot, but today I also had a tour to give and guests to entertain. Tomorrow was the full moon, and this weekend I had to be the alpha. If I played my cards right, maybe I could convince Fern's parents they wanted to return to Tennessee so my parents could come home.

Next week would be all studying every day. Maybe I could hide in the library when I wasn't in lectures—somewhere no one would find me.

Is there such a thing?

As the last class ended, Hollis took my bookbag so I could head right to the tour. I only had about ten minutes to make the run to the Union.

Breathing hard, I looked over the list of names and stifled a groan when I saw Ronald and Amy Meadows. Part of me knew Amy wanted to reconnect with the University and Ronald didn't know the campus, but this was my way to be a normal student. It was hard to disconnect from my werewolf life when werewolves kept invading my job.

Deciding to pretend I didn't even know them, I checked them in along with everyone else, plastered on a smile, and began my speech. This job was my way to stay connected to school as a student. So much of my life had been taken over by the pack and being an alpha. I didn't want to lose this small piece of being a teenager that was totally college.

Questions started to come in, and my body relaxed as I answered them. We moved through the streets as I talked about the buildings, dorms, city and classes. The tour headed towards Library Mall. On the way there, we passed a nature area near the lake with barren trees.

The scent was the first thing to hit me.

Before I could say anything, one of the people on the tour screamed. Another gasped. A third exclaimed, "Oh, my God! There's a dead body!"

Ronald came up to me and spoke quietly. "There's stench of wolf all over the place. Can you smell it?"

"Of course I can." I tried not to snap, but if the odor wasn't male and if Trista wasn't dead, I would think it was her.

Chapter 24 – Recurring Nightmare

My body trembled with anger, though I tried to hide it. "Please stay calm, everyone. I'm going to call the police. They may want to question any one of us. I'd like to ask you to stay." My voice was steady and commanding. The people on the tour looked at me and nodded, huddling closer.

I pulled out my phone and turned. Behind me, I found Ronald and Amy. In a voice low enough that they'd be the only ones to hear, I added, "Please text Tanner and let him know."

Amy nodded as I dialed 911. Once I'd finished my call, I sent a text to Easton to inform him as well.

It didn't take long for the police to arrive. They spoke to my clients and, after collecting their names, contact information, and statements, let them go. There was little chance any of them were connected to the crime.

Before they shuffled off, I handed each of them a card for a free tour. It wasn't their fault this one had ended so poorly.

As the police spoke to, and dismissed, each of the people, Tanner and Easton showed up. Tanner was held behind a line, but Easton was in uniform and allowed through. He started doing ... police things. He eventually came up to me and spoke softly. "Did you notice the victim has the smell of her ... but not her, all over him?"

"Yeah. We thought it was over, got lazy, and forgot to follow through. Once I get dismissed I'm heading home and calling a meeting."

"Good."

It took another hour to get through everyone. I demanded to be last. Once I was dismissed, I found Ronald and Amy waiting for me. We walked in silence until we got to the car. Then Ronald said, "Tell me about the scent."

As we drove to the pack house, I told them a story about the lone wolves that had invaded our territory. I explained that they'd started out in California and our theory as to why they'd come to Wisconsin.

Amy sighed. "Wow, that whole group sounds like they needed help. And those kids. Brought up in such lies and hate. I can't imagine it."

We'd arrived home.

Inside, we found the others waiting. They'd heard about the dead body. Until we could get more information from the police or Stone Security, there wasn't anything we could do. We were at a standstill.

Chapter 25 – Let's Get Furry

Friday morning was warm. The house was full of people, and they all looked to me for leadership. The best thing about the training program was the way it helped me to destress. I got to the gym and started to move. Luna was the next to join me. Then, after a few minutes, Conner and Dayna. I was a bit surprised when Hollis and Fern joined us, as well as Fern's parents.

The gym was big, and it would be getting its own workout today.

When I started to stretch, Hollis flopped down next to me. "I am so excited and scared and thrilled and terrified and ... I don't know, maybe numb. Can I be all of those things?"

A laugh bubbled out of me. "Well, you *are* all of those things so I guess you *can* be." I stretched out my legs, facing her and she did the same. We clasped hands and took turns leaning forwards and backwards to get deep leg stretches.

The others ran, did weights, used the exercise machines, and stayed in their own world.

Leaning back as she pulled me forward, Hollis said, "Tell me about today again."

She'd heard this several times, but it never hurt to hear it again. "After lunch, a meal that I want both you and Fern to eat more than you're used to eating, we'll head out to the back yard. I'll try to call your wolf while Luna tries to call Fern's. I want Luna to get a feel for this part of being an alpha and since we have two of you, it only seems fair."

Hollis nodded. "Okay, then we're both wolves. Then we run and play? Like, until tomorrow?"

"Ideally, yes. At first to get the feel of your paws under you, then as the rest of the pack comes, the others will join you, meet your wolves, and we'll all head out for our moon run."

"Yep, excited and terrified."

With a wink, I stood. "Well, I'm off to shower and get the morning started."

After my shower, I found Tanner and Tyler in the kitchen. I narrowed my eyes at them and grabbed a large mug of coffee. My stomach growled at me, letting me know it wanted more.

There was a box of muffins on the counter, I selected an apple one and sat. "Is this a social visit, or do we have news about yesterday's fiasco?"

Tyler leaned back. "A bit of both. My people have been watching Trista's brother, Torrance. From what we know, he hasn't left Oklahoma. I'm going to get someone to check in with his boss."

"How do you do that without it being suspicious?" I bit into my muffin and sighed.

"We call as if he's a reference for a job. Most people will give more information if that's what you're calling for." Tyler shrugged, finished his breakfast, and stood to get more coffee.

He looked in the cupboard for a travel mug. "Anyway, I'm heading back to work to look further into this. I just wanted you to get the preliminary report."

"Thank you."

After he left, Tanner leaned back. "It has to be the brother. He must've slipped out of the South and came up here. Vendettas are the name of the game with this family."

"I agree."

By mid-afternoon, more of the pack had showed up. About half of the people worked and wouldn't come until dinner time or later, but that left the other half available to come, hang out, and be together. This was my favorite part of pack ... being a family.

There were people in the living room, kitchen, dining room, and basement. Everyone was relaxed and happy. Helen and Conner cooked. They'd never cooked together before, but they seemed to be figuring it out.

Luna, Hollis, Fern, and I headed to the back yard. Thankfully, it was a nice day for their shift. During March in Wisconsin, the temperature could be anywhere from near summer temperatures to a blizzard. We had high spring, low rain weather, perfect for the day and night.

"Okay, Luna. Once Hollis is in position, I'm going to look deeply into her eyes and try to find her wolf. I'll release a bit of my mantle, but not too much. Then, in a commanding voice, I'm going to tell her wolf to shift. If all goes well, this will start the process. We also get to watch for the attack at the end, though with Fern, there may not be one."

"Because they're epsilon?"

"Yep." I smiled encouragingly.

"Got it."

Hollis trembled as she stripped and got into position. I knelt in front of her, lifted her chin, and asked her wolf to come out and play. I could feel Luna's attention on me as if she were studying for a class.

Once the shift began, Luna repeated the steps with Fern.

Fern was transgender and though they went by they/them pronouns, they'd been assigned male at birth. If they could choose, their body would be more feminine. We'd discussed it some. They'd known about what had happened with Bevin and Maddy, two trans wolves who lived out in California. I warned them it may not happen right away. It may take a few steps to get there.

Just like with Bevin and Maddy, when Fern's wolf completed the shift, their wolf reflected who they knew themself to be. In this case, Fern's wolf was female, as was Hollis's, though, that had never been in question.

Before they could run off, Ronald and Amy came out of the house. They both headed over to Fern and Amy cheered. "My goodness, you're a fierce-looking wolf. Where did your black fur come from?"

Fern yipped, then ran over to Hollis and rubbed up against her. As they ran, the white ring of Fern's tail showed the one part of the wolf that wasn't pure black. Hollis's red fur glowed in the sun; the black markings around her legs and midsection looked like shadows.

As I watched my friends, I spoke to Luna. "They're both so new and don't know their way around the area. And, with the new threat, I don't know if I want them running alone. I think I should shift and head out with them. If I do that, you're the only alpha in the house. Are you okay with that?"

Luna hesitated for only a beat, but I saw out of the corner of my vision her determination. Before she could answer, Ronald placed a hand on my shoulder. "No, you should be here ... both of you should. Amy and I will shift."

"You two don't know the woods."

Amy laughed. "I used to know them quite well, and I think we'll do fine. We've run in foreign woods before. Let us take Fern and their friend out. I think we need this."

The desire they felt to be with family was palpable. Luna and I retreated back into the house, giving them time to stretch muscles and bond as wolves before the full pack headed out together.

As the day wore on, the intensity I felt in my connection with the other pack members returned. I knew where everyone was, including Hollis and Fern, though Fern was a bit hazier. Since Luna had drawn them out, they'd be with Luna unless we made a change. I could feel the joy Hollis felt in her first run.

Before the full pack went out for a hunt, Tyler found me again. "Can we talk for a few minutes?"

"Yeah, of course." We headed to the office with Tanner and Luna.

Once the door was shut, Tyler sighed. "It took half the day to get a hold of this organization; they are very disorganized. I could talk with people but getting a specific person on the line was a near impossibility." He slumped. "It seems Torrance May had a death in his family. He requested some time off because he was the only family member able to put the deceased's affairs in order and had to travel."

"Well, at least that answers a few questions," I said, frustration lacing my voice.

"Do we know when he left Oklahoma?" Luna asked.

Tyler consulted his phone. "According to his job, the family member died last week Saturday, he found out Sunday, came in early Monday to get a few things in order and had a flight out of town Monday afternoon." He looked at something else. "They said he was flying to New York, where the family member had lived ... upstate New York."

I gazed up at the ceiling. "I wonder if anyone in this family knew how to tell the truth."

Tanner grumbled. "Doubt it."

Soon everyone from the pack arrived, and we all headed out to howl to the moon. Shifting felt like putting on my other natural skin. It hurt but felt oddly good. As we ran, Luna sent me images of flowers and trees she saw along her run. I sent images of the sky, wolves, and flowers in bloom. We both kept telling each other thoughts about our own adventure and ideas we had on where we should go.

As a pack, we didn't take down anything big. We did find a group of wild turkeys and brought down three of them. Running home, the warmer air felt cool and delightful combing through my fur.

For years—my whole life really—I'd come home and sleep in the tree house. Now that I was alpha, I wasn't sure hiding in the small house felt appropriate. I found a spot near the center of the yard and curled up for the night. Luna, Hollis, Fern, and Conner joined me. Before I fell asleep, I gazed at the wolves curled up in the back yard around me and a sense of purpose and joy settled over me like a blanket.

Chapter 26 – Message In A Bottle

The first full moon I'd ever run was one with my parents ... my biological ones. It took years for me to remember, for me to unpack the trauma of first them attacking me, and then them driving around the country with me trying to come up with a plan.

When I was five, when they'd been killed, we'd been stopped on the side of the road near Chicago. What took several years for me to piece together was that they'd been the ones to attack me as soon as we'd left Santa Fe. They'd done it that very first night. There'd been a full moon. *They'd pulled me from the car ... had they wanted to change me?* A shiver ran down my body.

From there, we'd driven first towards an ocean. My parents had talked about seeing an amusement park with candy and rides. There had been mountains and smelly hotel rooms. They kept on fighting about where they wanted to go and when they should go back home. They kept talking about threatening emails from someone claiming their life had been ruined by my parents.

Dad kept snarling that he could take care of it if they'd just return home.

The whole time, I tried to keep quiet in the back of the car. I knew making noise would mean I'd get in trouble. It was a lesson I'd learned in the past.

Then, one night, they pulled me from the car. The moon was big and took up my entire sight. I couldn't look away. My mom took off my clothes, at least, I'm pretty sure she did, because I never had to struggle with clothes. Then there was pain ... so much pain. With the pain was a sense of sorrow, not my sorrow, but the emotions of another soul that wanted to protect me. It confused me, I didn't understand what was happening. It almost felt like that other soul told me to sleep and it would protect me.

"She's so small. Do you think she'll be able to hunt?"

"She's a predator. Let's shift and run. A family ... a *true* family, dear. We'll be unstoppable."

Two nights later, we were stopped and a man killed them. Once he realized I was in the car, he unstrapped me and left me on the side of a huge road, alone and terrified.

A warm hand rubbed my arm. Love and support infused me. The image of me somehow looking strong and powerful cascaded through my mind in a series of images. Rolling my head to the side, I slit my eyes open and saw Luna gazing at me.

She smiled. "I don't know if you meant to share all of that, but I can't imagine living that way. Family is supposed to love you."

With a groan, I pushed myself up and found clothes. Luna followed suit and we made our way into the kitchen. Others were stirring, but we were the first out of the back yard. As was often the case, Helen was up and making breakfast. I poured two mugs of coffee and mumbled, "My room?"

Luna nodded.

We both sat on my bed, legs touching. "I can't believe you saw all that."

A laugh softly bubbled from her. "You were emoting pretty loudly. I think the connection between us is especially strong with our emotions ... and the moon. What caused the memory?"

The warm mug of magical brew eased something deep within me. Helen always made the best coffee in the pack. Jade once told me it was because she added a cinnamon stick to the beans in the grinder, but I'd tried that, and it still was never as good.

Once my soul felt a bit more settled, I relaxed and shut my eyes, thinking about waking up. "Waking up this morning, or, rather, when we returned last night. I've always ended up in the tree house. It symbolized safety. But we're the alphas. I thought ..." I sighed and sipped my coffee, wondering how silly this sounded. "I decided when we got home that we should be out amongst the pack ... family."

Luna reached over and placed her hand on my thigh and rubbed lightly. The touch of pack. The touch of alpha. The touch of my mate? My breathing smoothed out even as my confusion ramped up. I continued. "When I woke up this morning I could feel the cool grass beneath me. There has only been one other shift in my life when I woke up with grass under me."

Luna's hand stopped. "That first time, with your parents. Back when you were five. Did you remember it before this morning?"

I squeezed my eyes tighter, then opened them, looking over to gaze into her amazingly beautiful stormy and concerned look. The sides of my mouth quirked up. "Parts of it, but nothing that detailed. I think our connection has helped my memories open up."

"I wonder why." She continued to gaze at me.

My smile widened. "You really don't know?"

"No. Why would I? Do you?" Her eyes narrowed.

Contemplating what to say, I sipped my coffee, then I shrugged. In for a penny and all that. "My wolf knows I'm safe ... I know I'm safe. I can finally face the last of my demons."

Her jaw dropped. "But, Pebble, you have this amazing family. You could've told them at any time. You've been safe for years."

Warmth filled me thinking about my life ever since I walked into that conference room and saw Jade sitting there, eyes focused on me. I had my first premonition that day when I saw her, though I didn't know that for years. A vision of her and Owen, who I hadn't met yet flowed through my head and the words: *safety, family, go.*

"They saved me from the bigger picture, but it took the wolf longer to fully open up and become everything she could be. By then Jade and Owen had moved out. As much as I love my parents, my wolf told my five-year-old self that Jade and Owen were my true safe place. Also, by the time these memories were surfacing, there really wasn't a good time to share."

"Will you tell them now?" Luna's hand slipped to mine and squeezed.

"Yeah, I think so. They deserve to know. The next time the family is all together, I'll give them the full story. It'll be a gift for them to learn the final pieces."

Leaning over, Luna gave me a hug.

Most of the pack hung out for the day. It was Saturday and only a few had weekend jobs. Having a full house centered me in a way few things could. I asked Chris and Andy to pick up Thai food for lunch. After the memory crash of the morning, I needed the soul-soothing meal.

The scents filled the house as people ate where they could find a place to sit. Hollis and Fern sat with Fern's parents at the kitchen table. Luna, Dayna, and I were at the counter.

"It was ... weird. I had no idea that being a—" Hollis lowered her voice as if saying a naughty word, "—werewolf," then her voice returned to its normal level, "meant so much more. Like you said my smelling and hearing would be better ... but who knew?"

There were small chuckles from pack members in the living room. Those of us in the kitchen just smiled.

"That reminds me. We need to get to the mall this afternoon, maybe go to that movie everyone is saying is a real tear-jerker."

Conner came up behind me and put his hands on my shoulder. "Or you could rent a movie. With so many of us here, that could work as well."

Ronald nodded. "That's true. If we had a pack movie night, that could test out their boundaries. Both Fern and Hollis are new wolves and need sensitivity training. With classes starting up Monday, there's really no time to waste."

With a groan, Fern rubbed their face. "There was something else I had hoped to do today, but maybe over spring break would be better."

I narrowed my eyes at them and thought. "Do I *know* what you were hoping?"

They slowly nodded. "Probably. Growing up in a pack with Bevin and knowing about Maddy, you probably do. I just ... I need some help. Jade gave me the theory. I just need someone with two animals to help me."

Luna looked up. "Well, I'm your gal. What do you need?"

"Are you sure? It may not be comfortable."

Luna's face hardened. "I said I was your gal."

Trembling, Fern and Luna headed to the back yard, followed by Hollis. I patted Conner's hands. "They may need you."

He nodded. "Yeah, okay. You're right. If this is what I think it is, even just to guide them." His eyes looked a bit wild. "I'll head out with them."

Once the four of them had left, Ronald narrowed his eyes on me. "Do you think the wolf can do it? Fern is nonbinary, but has always wanted what Maddy has, a more female-presenting body."

"I don't know. Everything about our world is magical. All I can do is hope."

The process would take some time. First they'd have to explain to the wolf what they wanted. Then Fern would have to shift, run, and shift back. Being a new wolf, none of that would be quick.

I filled my plate with more food.

The front door opened, and Easton came in. Being a police officer, he was one of the people who'd had to head into work. Since he was monitoring the case of the body found on my tour, I wasn't too upset about his diligence. The fact that he was back so soon confused me.

He walked up to me and leaned on the counter, picking food from my plate. He moaned. "Gods, that's good. Okay, first, the police found a note in the tourist's pocket."

My brow furrowed. "A note?"

As we spoke, Tanner and Clare came in from the dining and living rooms.

"It was typed, folded, and stuffed in. No fingerprints have been found. I got a picture of the note." He pulled out his phone and showed us.

You and yours destroyed everything that was good in my life. Now I will return the favor. I will leave no STONE or PEBBLE unharmed.

A shiver of dread snaked down my body. "Do the police think this has to do with me?"

Easton shook his head. "You gave them the name Penelope Stone since that's what you use at your job. Smart, by the way. If they had Pebble Stone they'd be a bit more suspicious."

Tanner narrowed his eyes on his son. "Okay, but why drive all the way over here?"

"Another body was found. I didn't want to call or text. It's near the city pool and I figured I could drive here quickly on my way to the scene. I'm going to check for a note."

Tanner nodded. "I'll follow. You can let me know."

While we waited, a tension filled the house. Trista's brother had just declared he was in town and after the pack ... or at least after me and my family.

Andy and Chris came up to me, squeezing me in a hug. I instantly relaxed. The feel of a submissive wolf, much less two, was powerful. I rested my head on Chris's chest. "Thank you."

He made a superior sounding huff. "It's what we do."

Once they'd decided I was better, they headed back to a couch.

An exuberance shot through my being from Hollis, and I snapped my attention in the direction of the back yard.

The back door slid open, and the group came in. Fern's eyes shone and their hands trembled. When they got to the kitchen, their gaze jumped between me and their parents. "Oh, my gods ... I can't believe it ... It worked."

Chapter 27 – Task Force

The emotional rollercoaster ride would likely kill me. I ran to Fern and gave them a hug. They felt a bit different and smelled a lot different. Pulling back, I smiled at them. "Well, my friend. You'll have to learn a few things. I hope you're ready for that."

They blanched. "Gods, I hadn't ... oh."

Hollis grabbed their hand. "Don't worry. You've been teaching me for weeks, this is something I can teach you."

Once they'd headed to Fern's room, I sat heavily on a stool at the kitchen island. "Luna, I need to catch you up on everything. I also want to take some notes to keep track of all the things." I searched for Clare. She was in the living room but paying attention. "Do you want to head up to the office and discuss next steps?"

She nodded.

At the table, Ronald grumbled. "If you don't mind, I'd like to be included in this talk."

I thought about the implications, but since I wanted him and Amy to take over as the Tennessee alphas, this seemed like a good thing. "Amy, you too?" She nodded.

We headed up to the office. Once there, I filled Luna in on what she'd missed. "We need to let the other alphas know. I'm going to set up a meeting for tomorrow night. Hopefully we'll have information about today's hit."

Clare leaned forward. "Have you thought about all of you kids relocating to pack house until this is resolved?"

My face scrunched up, and I closed my eyes. "Honestly, no. Hollis and I already room together and Fern can move in. That puts three of us in one room, including an alpha."

Luna nodded. "Same with me and Dayna. And Conner could bunk out on our floor. We have men's and women's bathrooms down the hall from us. No one would blink an eye, really. I mean, we'd have to be subtle, but it'd be fine. I see random people in the wrong rooms a lot. If anyone asks, I'll just say he's our cousin. So, again, three of us in one room with an alpha."

The scent of the adults became cinnamon, cumin, and mint. They were skeptical and frustrated. Despite that, we were the alphas and could make the final call.

Ronald's mouth tightened and then he said softly, "I don't like this. If he's after you ... Living in the dorms, you have no protection."

"I disagree," I snapped back. "It's not easy to get into the dorms. They're locked and monitored. Then he'd have to know my dorm room and need to get past three of us. Two of us know how to fight."

With a scowl on his face, Ronald ground out, "I formally request permission to remain here until this situation is resolved."

It took an effort, but I kept a flat face. Luna placed a hand on my leg, and I felt her acceptance through our bond. It was hard to keep a neutral face when all the rules around me kept changing. Unclenching my jaw, I nodded slowly and said, "Request granted."

Before anyone could say anything more, my phone buzzed. I pulled it from my pocket and opened up the text messages. Tanner had sent two texts. I read them aloud to the group. "The second body is a young woman, again a tourist. She had a note."

Next to me, Luna's voice was low. "What does it say?"

Any left in Wisconsin are at risk. FERN on a STONE only gives away its position.

If Torrance thought threatening Fern's family would get them to tuck tail and run, he had miscalculated. The words of the second note lit a fire behind both Ronald's and Amy's eyes.

It took until the next morning to have a meeting with Easton and Tanner. We all returned to the office. Easton shook his head. "The police think this person is poorly educated from the bad grammar and obsessed with nature. They want to call him the 'Nature Killer.'"

"Gah!" I groaned but couldn't hold back a small snort. "They want to give him a name? No way. It'll legitimize him. We have to stop him."

Tanner wanted to discuss where all the college students would be living while this situation was going down, but we filled him in on our decision from the night before. He didn't like it but decided with three in each room he'd only grumble. Since I was pretty sure that was one of his favorite love languages, I let it slide off my back.

"Not to mention," I noted, "right now he's just going after tourists. Which is weird, right? We need to send a team to Trista's old apartment, check it out."

Tanner nodded. "I sent Greg, Andy, and Fred there this morning."

I nodded. "Okay, sounds good."

Easton's phone buzzed and he groaned. "I got off at three this morning, why is work contacting me?"

He looked at his phone and slumped. "Another body was found by the zoo at two. I wasn't called in because they decided even I needed some down time." He rubbed his eyes. "Another note." He yawned and shook his head, he obviously hadn't gotten enough sleep. "The Jewel of the pack with a Pied Piper of a Tree might have harassed those of mine but just wait and see."

Terror flowed through me like cold ice. "Tanner. I want Julez, Piper, and Spruce relocated here. They aren't the strongest fighters or the highest ranking wolves." A tension built within me. "Ronald, Amy, you'll be living here, so there will be others here at most times. And Easton is living here." As I spoke, I took notes. "Tanner, I need you to set up two person sweeps around the neighborhood patrolling quadrants. We will not let this person ... this group ... this whatever, defeat us."

Gazing at the ceiling, Tanner nodded. "Okay, that sounds like a plan."

Luna cleared her throat. "We should tell the others of the pack that anyone else can move in as well. If they're worried."

"I'll activate the calling tree once I contact Piper." I reached out and clasped hands with her. She'd made a good point.

Amy let out a breath. "And you have a meeting with the other alphas at eight?"

"No, four. It's early, but everyone was free. I told them I wanted to get back to studying but this was important."

She shut her eyes. "Can Ronny and I sit in and listen?"

Protocol said no, but in my heart this was them taking another step towards their alpha-hood. "Yes."

The others in the room gaped, but no one said anything.

When four o'clock rolled around, Luna and I sat behind the desk in full view of the computer's camera. Amy and Ronald were on the other side. The first to log in were my parents. They joined fifteen minutes early, but then a minute later Bevin's and José's faces popped into the meeting.

My body drooped on seeing the people I loved who were scattered around the world. "Before I start, I want to tell all of you how much I miss you and love you. Also, I told the Meadows they could listen in."

Bevin and José looked confused, but Mom and Dad smiled. Mom said, "Good idea. Ronny, if you can, stay quiet. I don't think the others should know. Did Fern shift?"

He chuckled. "They did, and with the magic your daughter taught them and Conner ... my gods, Hazel, these epsilon wolves."

At that, Bevin and José laughed.

Mom leaned in. "So, Pebble, last Wednesday, what did you do for your birthday? We sent a text, but you never replied."

Bevin's eyes narrowed. "Same."

The ginger scent of shock came from the other three wolves in the room. Luna slapped my arm. "Your birthday was this week, and you didn't tell me?" Then her eyes got wider. "Wait, did you do something with Hollis?"

I rubbed my face. "Ronald and Amy came in on Wednesday and Thursday was the full moon. I just ... it didn't seem to be high priority. Everyone had other things ... bigger things, to focus on."

Mom's face hardened and Dad shook his head. "Applesauce, pack is family, and they need to celebrate, especially things connected to their alphas."

Leaning back, I wasn't sure what to say. Bevin gave me a small smile. "I agree with your parents. Find a time to let loose. It's your last year as a teen. You need to have some fun."

Luna's face had a determined glint to it. "Don't worry. I'll make sure this happens."

The others smiled at what sounded to me like a threat. We spent the remaining minutes catching up on the good news of the pack.

As the other alphas logged in, Ronald and Amy leaned back and stayed silent. It took about ten minutes to explain our theory about Torrance and the three notes.

Frank, from Colorado, asked, "Do you think we're all in danger? Should we all be at high alert?"

Luna shook her head. "Only if we can't contain this. I believe he's after us because we took out his sister and her gang. He had to collect or create a gang before he could come up here. Now he's half-mad."

"Or all mad," I added.

She nodded. "And trying to rile us. His notes are meant to scare us, get us off our game, but all they're really accomplishing is letting us know exactly who's after us. We're coming together and we'll find him." She shook her head. "The whole family is off their rocker. They think they're a lot cleverer than they are."

The Massachusetts alpha, Finley, nodded. "That sounds right. Thank you for contacting us right away. You two are new, but you're doing the right things, from protecting your pack to keeping the lines of communication open. When you first called this, I worried you were too quick to make this call, and I was wrong."

The others who didn't know us nodded. There were a few other announcements as long as everyone was there, and then the call ended.

When we got to the living room, everyone waited. I could smell Hollis's worry. "Wow, did I choose the wrong time to become a wolf."

Ronald laughed. "I don't know, these idiots don't care what you are. Being associated with us is enough. Trista saw you here and Torrance probably has your name. He probably doesn't know you're a wolf. Now you can run faster. I think you chose the right time."

She gazed at me, mouth gaped open. "Is this why you could always beat me in races? You cheated?"

Chapter 28 – Learning From The Best

On Monday, I was distracted, and it was hard to follow my one and only class. It being Spanish didn't help. As I trudged from my lesson, I knew I'd need Hollis's help to reteach whatever it was the professor had explained. My only saving grace was my ability to take good notes. I was pretty sure everything the professor had put on the board was in my notebook.

When I got back to the dorm, it felt tight with three people's stuff.

I sat on my bed, knees to my chest, back to the wall, and massaged my temples. It was the first time I'd been alone in a long time, and it felt good. I knew it wouldn't last, but I tried to pull the quiet into myself.

Before I managed any sort of peace, my phone buzzed. My first instinct was to turn it off or throw it across the room. It hadn't brought me anything but frustration. Instead, I checked and saw a message from Easton. Another death. This one was obviously done by an animal. No note, so the police believed it was a different suspect. However, Easton knew better … same scent.

When Hollis got back to the room, she found me pacing. I'd given up on finding any sort of calm.

"You okay?"

"I have a big exam in Spanish at the end of the week, and I didn't understand a word the professor said. When I got back here, Easton texted that he found another one. I don't know how I'm going to do this. But, on the bright side, I no longer have to hide any of my life from my best friend, and that is really freaking amazing."

She hugged me and all the tranquility that had slipped through my fingers all morning settled on me like a blanket. I sunk into the hug and sighed. It felt like the pieces of the puzzle that made me up were realigning. I hadn't felt this complete since …

My eyes widened and I gaped at her. "You're submissive."

We hadn't done a check because we had two new wolves and so much going on. Also, new wolves were zeta and it was customary to wait until the second or third run, but, gods above …

Her eyes widened. "Is that bad?"

"No, that's—" I pulled her in for one more hug and felt complete contentment fall over me. "Thank you. Gods above, I needed that. Let's study."

"You sound less frantic." Her head tilted and she studied my face.

"Of course I do, my best friend in the world is a submissive wolf, the heart of the pack. The one who brings stability to us all." One of my eyebrows rose.

"Oh!" Her mouth formed a perfect 'O.' "That's cool. So, I can make you less frantic?"

"I mean, you've kind of been doing that my whole life, right?"

Her eyes narrowed and she gazed up at the ceiling. "I have, haven't I?"

"Well, you have more power to do that now."

"That's cool!"

We went to the common room, which had big tables and less clutter, and worked on Spanish for a few hours. Eventually, Fern joined us.

When they heard the news about Hollis, they smirked. "I'm not surprised at all. Look at the three of us. The Three Musketeers of amazing."

I snorted. I wasn't sure how I'd ended up with these people in my life, but I was keeping them.

Tuesday was a long day of classes and studying. Every day we had an exam or paper due before spring break. All six of us got together to study in the library. If anyone thought to attack us, they'd be in for a big surprise.

The first of the big midterms came on Wednesday. Com Arts had presentations scheduled for a couple of sessions, and I had to give mine on the first day. I was used to speaking in front of people. As it went, most of the students had time to present on Wednesday, with a few stragglers on Thursday before the exam. I presented on pronghorns, using the research we'd done over winter break.

Gods, was the trip only last semester? It feels like it was a lifetime ago.

After class, I met with the others for lunch. A text came in from Piper. *You're needed at home. It's an emergency. Bring Fern and Conner if they're with you. Hurry!*

It shook me. I called Piper back. "Oh! You aren't in class, good."

"None of us are, we're eating lunch. Should we get a cab?"

"No, I'll come in a pack SUV. Just tell me where to pick you up." She sounded distracted.

"Is everything okay?" Worry coursed through me.

"I'll be there in fifteen minutes. Be waiting outside." She hung up before I could ask anything else.

I shrugged at the others as frustration surged through me, but we finished up and headed out to meet Piper. Less than a half-hour later—Piper pushed her speed—we were home.

Aunt Allison came out of the medical suite. "I know Piper didn't tell you much."

"No, she didn't say a word."

Piper sighed. "I didn't know what to say."

"There was an attack. There isn't much to know. I fear if she doesn't get help with her healing, it may be too much for her wolf ... but I really don't know."

Fern gasped, and chills ran throughout my body.

Aunt Allison put a hand on each of us, calming us as only a submissive could. "Amy needs help. I was hoping—" She looked at Fern and Conner. "I know you're both epsilon wolves and you can lend your wolf to help with the healing. Moreover, Fern, I know you have some experience with healing, and you can help more."

I shook my head. As much as this hurt me inside, they were both new wolves. This was asking too much. "No. Jade can only do that because she has two animals. I remember the early story of her healing Janet. Both her animals helped, and she nearly died herself."

Fern's face was pale. "It's my mom, Pebble. What do I need to do?"

Anger surged in me. "You need a second animal, that's what you need."

Hollis wrapped arms around me from behind and Luna clasped my hand. They were double-teaming me.

Aunt Allison smiled weakly. "First, you need to eat. More than you've ever eaten. Then you need to promise that when Conner tells you to back off, you'll listen. Pebble is right, you won't be able to self-heal or self-monitor if you're helping your mom."

"Food. Willing to listen to Conner. I can agree to that."

"We will be monitoring you, so you'll have to pull out when we tell you to." My voice was hard, laced with alpha. "This isn't a case of trading you for your mom, Fern."

From the living room, Ronald growled low. "Do not kill yourself for your mom. She wouldn't thank you ... but if you can, help her."

Looking like they'd been punched, but with a sense of determination, Fern headed to the kitchen where the counter was filled with cheese, crackers, sausage, yogurt, and a Tanner shake. I looked at the last longingly.

From behind me, I heard a chuckle. "I can make another one, boss."

I gazed up at him. "Fern may need more than one."

He nodded and headed over to the blender.

After Fern ate as much as they could, we all headed into the medical room, Fern and I both drinking our chocolatey goodness. Luna took mine to share. I wasn't sure if I liked this part of being partnered up, but she just smirked at me as she handed it back.

Amy was on the medical cot and didn't look good. I dialed Jade and put her on speaker phone. She began to tell Fern exactly what to do.

Fern sat, put their hands on Amy's arm, and they shut their eyes.

From the phone, we heard Bevin. "Has Fern's breathing evened out? Do they look like they're in a trance?"

Aunt Allison smiled. "Yes, just like Jade the few times I've seen her healing."

"Good. Now, this is the tricky part. Watch the eyes and hands. With Jade, she kind of squeezes her eyes a bit and her hands tremble when she's low on energy. Those are her only tells."

There was a small gasp. "You never told me I had any tells."

Bevin laughed. "There was no reason. It was 'find a tell' or stand with a hand on your shoulder for hours on end."

She grunted. "Okay, that makes sense." In the background I could hear kids making loud, sharp, happy sounds. Then there was a crash. Jade sighed. "We should go. The kiddos are ruining the house."

I laughed. "Do you mean running *around* the house?"

"No." Bevin sighed, though he didn't really sound upset. "She doesn't. Five kids who can all move on their own. She means ruining the house ... tearing it down around us. We've met our match."

Aunt Allison laughed. "Once this is over, Jackson and I will fly out to snuggle and kiss each of those wonderful bundles."

"Yes!" Jade said with conviction. "We'd love to have you."

Bevin agreed. "Call if you need more help. We're always here for you, Pebble. You know that. You too, Luna. You don't know us well, but that doesn't mean we're not family."

Luna's eyes widened. "Um ..." She stammered. I'd never heard her stammer. "Thank you."

The call ended and we each took turns monitoring Fern. After three hours, I saw their hands start to tremble. "Conner! Come tell Fern to disengage."

He put a hand on their arm. At first, I saw Fern shaking their head, but then they slumped. When their eyes opened, I handed them a second chocolate shake. I knew as soon as their arm started to lift, they'd pushed too hard, and they'd never be able to hold the treat. Kneeling on the ground, I held the glass to their lips and helped them to get the much needed calories.

Once they'd drunk half the goodness, Fern sighed. "Gods above, that was intense. Mom's wolf was doing a lot, but my wolf and I, we both could help. It was trippy."

Ronald stood on the far side of the bed with Aunt Allison. "How is she?"

Fern smiled weakly. "I think she'll be okay. I wanted to do a few other things, but time should help ... or I can do more."

"No!" Luna, Conner, and I all said at the same time.

Aunt Allison smiled. "Her vitals are fine. I'll do a better checkup once you all clear out. It smells like pizza was ordered. Fern, you need to eat ... a lot more."

I moved to help them, but their dad got there first.

Over pizza, Fern still trembled, but they managed to eat. "I was so scared at first, but you all helped me stay calm, and even having Jade there, even though she was only a voice, it really helped. I know what you all meant by a second animal. Jade talked about leaving one behind to protect her; too bad Sarah isn't here to give me a panther."

"If you really want a panther, Kal, her maker, works at the University. We may be able to arrange it."

A stillness came over the kitchen. Then Conner cleared his throat. "I may want that too. I know I'm an engineering student, but my wolf knows how to heal."

Laughing, I just shook my head. How did I end up with the strangest pack in the country?

Chapter 29 – When Plans Come To Fruition

Thursday morning, I woke up and groaned. My head pounded. Fern moaned and their stomach growled. "I can't believe how hungry I am. Is this how your sister lives?"

That made me laugh. "Yes. All the time."

"Gods ... okay, food."

We got up and started to dress. Hollis woke up, grumbled, and also put on clothes. The three of us trudged down to the cafeteria. Once we had food, I rubbed my head. "Three exams. I have to survive three exams and the discussion is canceled. Then classes are over for a week."

Fern sipped their coffee and winced. "Did you text Kal?"

Despite my groggy state, I smiled. "I did. I'm hoping he'll get back to me today or tomorrow. If he agrees, and there's no guarantee he will, maybe you and Conner can become what Jade mostly is."

Hollis finished her first cup of coffee then bit her lip gazing down at her tray. She started to play with her food, eating it some, but mostly pushing it around the plate.

Fern reached over and rubbed her shoulder. "What's wrong?"

"I just ... do you wish this never happened? I know last semester when it was just you and your parents it was so much easier. Now you're juggling a lot. Do you wish I never found out?" At the end, she finally looked up into my eyes.

I knew this was an important question. We'd been friends since I joined her class halfway through the year in third grade. A scared awkward girl who'd never been to public school and barely knew how to act with kids my age. She'd been my friend and protector for ten years.

"When I was young, the first rule was to not tell anyone. Then I met you and all I wanted to do was share every secret I had. Mom and Dad spent a few nights really making sure I knew that it was wonderful I had a friend, but I had to be careful. We practiced what I could and couldn't tell you."

Hollis laughed. "No wonder you sometimes sounded so robotic when you spoke. I told everyone it was because you were scared, but it was more than that."

Fern chuckled with us. I nodded. "For years, I've wanted to bring you into this part of my life. I've also wanted to protect you. You deserve your own life, not mine. I knew you wanted to travel, and being part of a pack makes it harder ... not impossible, but not as easy. But to be honest with you, in my very selfish heart of mine, I'm thrilled. I no longer have to come up with cover stories about my family. You now know everything, which is really nice. You're even more like a sister to me."

At that, Hollis smiled, reaching across the table to give my hand a squeeze. "I really like that last bit. I get that travel will be harder, but I can still visit other places, right?"

"Of course. As a submissive, it'll be better if you have someone with you, but it'll also be easier because you won't be seen as a threat. But it's more dangerous as a wolf. Other wereanimals will smell it on you." I tilted my head to the side. "Well, maybe they won't. Thanks to the bears, we do have a solution to that. However, you now have more to think about. When you travel you have to find places to run, and if you are in another wolf's territory you need to check in. It's more work."

She nodded. "But us, we're good?"

Happiness bubbled in me, and Hollis lifted her head, gently sniffing. "Do I smell vanilla and citrus?"

That made me laugh. "Delight and excitement."

Her nose wrinkled. "That's better than most of the smells around here. And the calming feel of Fern is amazing. Going to classes has been rough, especially with everyone being worried about exams. But you're right, one more day and we're done."

"Okay, I'm off to prepare for Spanish ... you know, get in the right headspace." I moved around the table and kissed each of them on the cheek. "Wish me luck."

Hollis stood and gave me a hug. "You'll do great. I'm sure of it."

"Thank you. I'll see you both at lunch, then we can head home."

Hollis snorted. "I can't believe you're calling your home my home."

"Well, it's the pack den, it's everyone's home." I waggled my brows at her. "Mi casa es tu casa!" That much Spanish, I knew. Then I spun and headed to class.

By the end of my last exam, I wanted to sleep and cheer. The first year wasn't over, we were just at spring break, and we still had a few more weeks, but it was so close. I felt like college was already kicking my butt. What would the next three years bring?

Was all this stress from school, or was it the addition of pack duties?

On the way to the mess hall, I got a text from Easton. *Car on the way. Be ready to ride in twenty.*

I contacted the others, and they'd received the same.

I made it back to my dorm room in eight minutes, switched bags, and was down to meet Easton well within the time he gave. The others were there as well. I slid into the front seat. "Is there another death? Is there an emergency at home?"

Determination poured off him. "No, nothing like that. This time I have good news." He navigated campus, avoiding the other cars and students who either walked like zombies or zipped around, late for something. It was a bit of a mad rush until we were clear and close to home.

"Tell us! What's the news?"

"Well, we didn't find anything at Trista's place. It looked almost the same as the last time we were there. Despite that, the rent is still being paid. The landlord said it's Trista's ... Beth's until the end of July. Once we get this taken care of we're planning on searching it more thoroughly and seeing what we can find. We should've done that in February. Sorry about dropping the ball on that."

I shook my head. "We all overlooked a lot of things. It's a group mess-up."

"Well, if you remember, I placed a bunch of trackers on Trista's items."

Slowly nodding, I waited for him to continue. The trackers had been placed at her apartment. If no one had been there, that seemed to be a dead end. "Did you also put any cameras at her place?"

"We did, but they haven't shown any movement." His smile widened. "But one of the trackers went off this afternoon. Torrance had to have set it off. He's on the move and we know where he is."

Chapter 30 – Dissent In The Ranks

There were two big bowls of salad and three large chicken pot pies in the kitchen when we walked in. I nearly swooned. Next to me, Fern moaned.

In the other room, I could hear Amy chuckle. "Come, my teens. Eat before you faint dead away."

She didn't have to tell me twice.

We descended on the food, and it was as good as the last time she'd cooked. After a few bites, Hollis smiled shyly at Amy. "Fern told me how good this meal was and that it was their favorite. I can see why. This is amazing. Thank you for making it for us."

I grunted my agreement.

Luna elbowed me. "What Pebble means is, we thank you for feeding our pack. You didn't have to, and we very much appreciate it."

I grunted again, and Amy laughed.

Once I'd finished off my plate, I faced Tyler. "Do we know where the tracker is? Where Torrance landed?"

He shook his head. "We have a general idea, but Tanner is out getting a better location. He'll text us when he knows what's going on."

A low snarl escaped me. "Is he planning on doing clean-up while we're here? Protect us by doing the dirty work?" I looked around the room and it dawned on me that Clare, Ronald, and Easton were all gone.

The bitter scent of guilt came from Amy as Tyler shrugged. "I was just told he was off on a fact-finding mission and that he'd let us know what he found."

Annoyed, I faced Amy. "But you know more."

Her face tightened. "You all are children. It is our duty and pleasure to keep all of you safe. I know you're the alphas and strong. In my head it all makes sense, you're doing an amazing job, but in my heart ... Pebble, you're eighteen."

"I'm nineteen."

Fern slapped my shoulder with the back of my hand. "When did that happen? When was your birthday?"

Hollis checked her phone and slammed her forehead with the back of her hand. "Darn it all, how did I let that happen?"

Luna snarled. "We still need to discuss this. I'm debating either a full pack meeting or having a calendar added to the website."

"We are not changing the subject," I growled back.

"Yes, we are," Luna shot back, eyes practically glowing. "We don't know where the others went, and you can't control people not in our pack. So, we'll discuss something that will bring the pack joy."

I harrumphed. "When is yours?"

Her brow rose. "April thirteenth, if you must know."

My jaw was clenched tight, anger still heating my body at the thought I was being kept from helping to end this. Finally, Hollis got up and wrapped an arm around my shoulders, calming me regardless of what I wanted. When I still seethed, Conner closed his eyes and released a bit of epsilon calm.

Suddenly, I felt like I was floating on a cloud of happiness. My muscles relaxed and my breathing evened out. "Why is everyone conspiring against me right now?" Despite wanting to sound angry, my voice came out soft.

Luna leaned over and gave me a soft kiss. "Because we all love you and want our alpha to be safe. Let us care for you so *we* can continue to care for our pack."

The joy emanating from Hollis washed away the last of my anger. She gave my shoulder one last squeeze then went back to the table. As she sat she said, "Oh, and

Pebble's birthday was last week, March eleventh. I don't know how we all missed it."

Luna slowly turned her face a blank mask. "I do. That was the day Fern's parents came. The day before the full moon. We discussed this with her parents a bit. Trust me when I say that this isn't something that's going to continue to be ignored."

For some reason, her words didn't fill me with feelings of rainbows and butterflies.

The door opened before I could ask her what she was thinking. The group that had gone to track Torrance came in and joined us in the kitchen.

My anger grew again, and I glared at Tanner. I knew who the ring leader was. "You know my thoughts on this, Tanner."

He leaned on the far counter, ankles crossed, arms crossed, face tight. "I do. But we needed to follow fast. If you were here, we would've fought and disagreed on the outcome. Since you were in class, I made the executive decision. If we'd have waited, I don't know if Torrance and his goons would've still been traceable."

Part of me wanted to scream, but another part knew his reasoning was sound. After a moment to calm my breathing, I unclenched my jaw and gave him a curt nod. "Please report."

He blinked once then nodded. "We found Torrance with three others in a park. When we got there, he was pacing, and the others cowered. He yelled at them. 'Why didn't you find me anyone last night? How hard is it to get a college kid?'"

Tanner rubbed his face then dropped his head back, gazing up at the ceiling. "One of the men looked up and Torrance snarled. The man dropped to his stomach and shook. There was so much anger rolling off Torrance, he was ready to take out his people. If I were to guess, the goonies he has with him are newly changed."

Ronald grunted. "That was my take as well. They smelled terrified and overwhelmed."

Clare shook her head. "They were all half-wits. No one knew what was going on. We walked out, and Torrance saw us. He yelled at his men for letting us follow. Tanner laughed, one of his low and slow belly laughs, it was lovely. He explained to Torrance that we followed him, not the idiots on the ground."

Easton chuckled at the memory. "Then that imbecile attacked Clare, probably thinking she was our weak link. He yelled, 'This is for Beth.' His attack was clumsy. His men never moved from the ground, and we just watched ... Clare obviously didn't need help." Everyone in the group smirked. "The fight was short. Once it was over, his men shook worse than with Torrance."

Tanner growled low. "These lone wolves who rule with fear and ignorance piss me off."

His son nodded. "I questioned them, confirming they were newly made wolves and had no idea what Torrance was up to. They didn't want to be part of it but couldn't get away from him. They're all from Oklahoma but need a pack to train them."

All my muscles tensed, and I looked at each of them. There was no way we were bringing three wolves into our pack that had come to my city to kill. They'd been coerced, but their end game had been to bring us down.

Ronald cleared his throat, and my focus snapped to him. "I'm thinking of bringing them to Tennessee. I don't think they knew all of Torrance's plans, and that pack needs more wolves."

Everything in me tensed. "Are you saying what I think you're saying?"

A slow smile spread on his face. "It's been really nice being part of a pack. I forgot how much I missed being in a big messy family. Living alone, well, we got numb, but Amy and I have discussed it. We've decided it's time to go home."

Chapter 31 – The Beast Within

Thursday night we had a big pack dinner. Everyone came to celebrate what we hoped this time really was the end of the lone wolf invasion of our territory. We were also saying goodbye to Ronald and Amy who wanted to get to Tennessee as soon as they could. Now that they'd made up their minds, they had a lot to do to make the shift from Kentucky lone wolves to Tennessee alphas.

Julez gave a satisfied sigh. "I for one am excited to have Hazel and River back, but also sad. Pebble, you've done an amazing job, and Luna, I've been really impressed. I know, in a few years, when you two really do become our alphas, we will remain the best pack anywhere."

Fred smiled. "I agree. You two are young, but like my son out in California, the position of alpha fits both of you well."

Tanner grunted. "I could ask for a bit more listening to the adults—"

Everyone laughed and Clare said, "Then they wouldn't be alphas. They listened to us just as much as Hazel and River, and you know it. They heard our words, respected our position, and made their own decisions. They did exactly what alphas are supposed to do."

Chris whooted at the far end of the room. "That's my girl ... or gals!"

Luna stood. "I officially want to say that I am thrilled to be alpha of this pack for as long as you'll have me. I also want to thank Ronald and Amy Meadows for coming and helping out as we dealt with Torrance May. And lastly, I will remind the Meadows, Fern is our epsilon. They'll have a hard time getting Fern out of Wisconsin, parents or not." She winked at them. "We have Hollis and won't give her up either." Then she sat with a smirk.

The pack went wild, clapping and shouting their agreement. Fern blushed and their parents took the teasing good-naturedly.

On Saturday, I got out of the shower and dressed in jeans and a shirt that read, *Relax, we're all crazy, it's not a competition.* It was one that both Jade and I had owned multiple versions of. After the week of exams and the hopeful end of the lone wolf invasion, I was feeling a bit crazy. Also, in the back of my mind, I kept thinking about my parents.

Their return had me confused. The hope of going back to being just a student made my soul sing. The concept was freeing. At the same time, over the last three and a half months, Luna and I had done something huge. We'd forged something new and beautiful that I hoped would grow into what my parents had or what Bevin and José had.

It wasn't that I thought holding off on being the alphas would ruin what we were building, I just felt we'd figured out so much and I wanted to continue on our path ... not leave it.

Do I really want to be an alpha in college?

I sat on the edge of my bed and let the questions fill me.

Despite thinking I knew the answer, I decided to hold off any decisions until after I had coffee and food.

In the living room, I found ... everyone. My mouth fell open. "What are you all doing here? There isn't a pack meeting ... or a run." Gazing at the faces, I thought I saw every pack member milling about.

Chris, who sat with Andy on one of the love seats, smirked. "We got a message from our alpha. Apparently, someone turned nineteen and failed to mention it. We decided a day with the pack would be the best solution. And since the Dynasty is gone from our city—"

"State," Tanner rumbled from the kitchen.

"Right. State," Chris continued, undeterred. "We want to party like we're all teenagers."

Smiling at Chris, I sent an image of an anvil falling on a goose to Luna.

I heard her laughing in the kitchen right before the image of me falling on my butt after meeting her goose filled my head. I couldn't help it, I laughed.

Helen and Conner made pancakes, sausage, eggs, and fruit salad for breakfast. Then we went to play miniature golf. Apparently, Luna had reserved the entire place for the morning. From there, we went to an all-you-can-eat sushi restaurant.

As I filled my plate for the third time, I turned to Hollis. "I thought this place wasn't open for lunch on Saturdays. Haven't we bemoaned that in the past?"

She held up her hands. "Have you ever tried saying 'no' to Luna? She planned out a birthday day for you and that was that."

Our next stop was pack house. We went for a run. It wasn't often we could run as a pack on a non-full moon night. It felt different and my soul sang with joy. Next to me, Luna howled, her happiness flowing through the pack.

By the time we returned, shifted, and dressed, it was evening. Inside, the house smelled like Thai, and I nearly swooned. Everyone knew my favorite food, and many laughed at my reaction.

While I ate, people brought me small gifts. After handing me a chocolate shake, Tanner gave me a box. Inside was a mug that read, *It's not a shake, but it'll have to do.* I snorted. Hollis gave me half a necklace that said, 'sisters forever'.

Fern, Conner, and Dayna presented me with a gift certificate. Dayna said, "This is the place with the best cheese curds on State Street. This should cover dinner for two."

Luna gave me a box and smirked. I hesitated. The amusement she felt caught everyone's attention. Almost everyone else had given me something during the evening and I knew after this gift we'd get to the cake I'd already seen on the counter and my day of birthday celebrations would be done.

Trying not to make a skeptical face, and knowing I failed, I opened up the present. In it was a porcelain statue of a goose squawking at a girl who was halfway fallen on her butt. Her hands and legs were flung out wide and her face had a look of shock. The girl had short curly dark hair and green eyes.

It took me a second, but I threw my head back and howled. Though no one else in the pack knew about that day, the others joined in laughing. Goose decorations were such a thing for all of us that Luna had just cemented her place in the pack.

On Sunday morning, Kal came over. He'd received my text and met me for coffee on Saturday morning. He wasn't thrilled with the request, but he also wasn't against it.

Both Conner and Fern were nervous and excited. Aunt Allison was available for medical help, as was Helen, our resident nurse. Tanner and Clare were there to be muscles, as were me, Luna, and Dayna.

Though Ronald and Amy had wanted to stay, they felt following through on their decision to get to Tennessee was more important. They headed down on Friday and were going to spend most of our spring break moving their stuff.

We all sat around the kitchen table, eating sausages, eggs, and pancakes.

"So, Kal," I said, sipping my coffee. "When you bite someone who already has an animal, you have to be a bit more intense. It can't be anything casual. Five or six bites, not one or two."

His brow knit. "Hmm. I guess that makes sense. You have to get past the animal trying to heal their soulmate. Something simple would just be ignored."

I smiled. "Exactly. We'll have a bucket of water so you can wash out your mouth, or you can run out to the lake, which isn't frozen anymore."

He finished his meal. "That all sounds acceptable. This is a lot more than anything I've seen in the past. I know I created Jade and Sarah, but that was by accident. I've never actually done this on purpose."

Both Conner and Fern sat at the table, their nerves filling the room. Each of us took turns reminding them to eat. Finally, Aunt Allison shook her head. "Okay, enough torturing these two, let's just get it over with. I've witnessed this once, and never thought I'd see it happen again. However, to have a healer like Jade in the pack again—" She shook her head.

In the back yard, they each stripped down, Conner to shorts and Fern to shorts and a halter top. We'd set up two stretchers for them to lie down on.

Kal went behind one of the privacy screens and began his shift. It was fast. He was a strong werepanther and had done the shift many times in his life.

Once he was back, I squatted down next to him and repeated to him what everyone said to me. Several bites to each of them. Don't get the taste in your mouth. Rinse immediately afterwards. He knew all of this, but, as always, hearing it in animal form helped.

I preferred being on this side of the process.

Tanner and Luna stood over Fern, with Helen as the healer. I stood to stand next to Clare over Conner, with Aunt Allison as the healer. After a second, Kal dashed forward, chomping down hard and fast on first Fern: leg, leg, leg, belly, belly, and then Conner.

They both tensed with the pain. As often happened, they passed out. *Is that their animal protecting them from the pain in a situation they know they're safe in?*

We put a blanket over each of them and carried them to the medical suite. Aunt Allison cleaned the wounds and checked them over, but they both started healing right away.

A rotation was set up so that the two were never alone. It was ironic that the only two people who could've checked up on them were the two in the room.

Luna came in while I sat, watching them. I gazed up at her. "We should've done them separately, then we could've ... I don't know, done more?"

She rubbed my shoulders. "I don't think we could've convinced Kal to come here twice. Once he ran and shifted back, he looked pale. If I read the situation correctly, that's his last time doing anything like this."

I slumped. "You're probably right. Well, I hope it worked for their sakes."

"And ours."

A small laugh bubbled out of me. "Well, yeah, ours too. But packs have been surviving without double animals and without epsilons for generations. It's amazing having all these dual animals, but I just want our pack members whole and happy."

Monday morning, Fern woke up. They stretched and sighed. I was still in the room having napped in the chair. "Pebble, are you awake?"

I yawned. "Um, yes? How are you?"

They laughed. "I don't know. The last thing I remember was a black panther attacking me."

A low growl churned in my gut and Fern laughed harder. "Okay, okay, give me a second." They closed their eyes, and a smile spread across their face. "Gods, Pebble, she's fantastic. She's all black, except for a white diamond on her chest ... my chest."

Leaping up, I gave Fern a hug. "It worked? You have two animals?"

"It worked." They sighed gustily.

"Can you find out if it worked for Conner?"

He groaned. "It did. My black panther has white paws like my wolf. This is so weird." He opened his eyes and pushed himself up to sitting. "Jade talked about a mental landscape where she and her animals would sit and bond. Now I understand why. I sort of have that with the oceanscape, but I need to make it ... more."

I leaned back in my seat. "I'm going to have to send the two of you, and probably Hollis, to California this summer. You'll need some serious training. Not only are you two epsilon, but now you have two animals. Fern, get on writing that book!"

Fern laughed, and everyone's joy filled the room.

Chapter 32 – Spring Break

On Tuesday, Hollis, Fern, and I took a run as wolves. Fern and Conner hadn't shifted into panthers yet and would probably need Kal's help the first time. We'd wait until the full moon to do that.

I wanted the three of us to go out as friends, the original trio, and just have fun. I gloried in the feel of my paws digging into the dirt and leaves that littered the ground. The smell of the trees as new buds began to grow.

When we got to a fallen tree, I showed my friends, two new wolves, how to use their bodies to leap over the trunk.

At first, they both failed, tumbling and rolling on the ground. Hollis ended up with a twig in her fur and Fern was covered in leaves, which made me loll my tongue in a wolf laugh.

I waited patiently as they each tried again and again. Once they both figured out how to work their bodies to leap over the log, we continued to run. I got them to the lake and encouraged them to first look at the surface, gazing at their reflections, then we all splashed in to play.

Eventually, we were back to running, our bodies eating up the miles as we let our legs and muscles move.

At one point, the image of our run flashed in my head, three wolves—gray, red, and black—weaving through the woods, from above. Looking up, I saw a goose flying high above us. I tried to send a pulse of love and acceptance to the crazy, scary bird. I couldn't believe that my life had gotten to the point that there was a goose I wasn't completely terrified of.

Luna's amusement at my fear of geese filtered through our bond as my friends and I ran.

Wednesday morning, I sat on a couch in the living room reading the latest book by A. R. Grimes, one of my favorite authors. The door opened and before I knew it, I was hugging my parents.

"Mom! Dad! You're back!" The thrill of having them home infused me.

"We are, Applesauce. Glad to see your powers of observation are still acute." Dad smiled. "I'm also glad to know you're happy to see us."

The room started to fill with the others. Most didn't know my parents very well, but they would; they were the rightful alphas. It wouldn't take them long to realize how wonderful my parents were.

We headed to the kitchen and someone ordered Mexican food. Tanner came over. He probably missed Dad as much as I did. They were best friends. Aunt Allison and Uncle Jackson came over as well.

Uncle Jackson engulfed Mom in a hug. "Sis! You're back. You survived Tennessee. You must have stories to tell. When is the big pack meeting?"

Everyone laughed. We sat around eating tacos, burritos, rice, and beans.

Dad sighed. "I'm not going to call a pack meeting."

The noise of the table stopped. Tanner tilted his head. "River? Are you feeling okay?"

After selecting another taco, Dad waggled his eyebrows. "As a matter of fact, I'm feeling amazing. Do you know, this is the first time in," he checked his watch, even though I doubt it gave him any useful information, "years, lots and lots of years, that I don't have any responsibilities. Hazel and I discussed this on the drive up. We're going to go to the pack training location up north."

We all just looked at him. Aunt Allison smiled. "For how long?"

Mom sipped her soda. "Now, that's the question, isn't it? Pebble and Luna are doing a great job. They have dealt with an immense situation and handled it well. They have the respect of the pack. They did it all while keeping their grades up." Mom's eyes narrowed. "You *have* kept your grades up, haven't you?"

I nodded and Luna smirked and said, "Of course."

Mom gave a nod. "We've decided we need a vacation. So, we're going to move up to the training camp."

Uncle Jackson gave them a small smile. "But, River, what about Stone Security?"

"Tyler is doing great at running it and he's training Hannah. Fred and Clare's kids are going to take over the world. First the California pack, then one will take over Stone security in California, the other here in Wisconsin." He laughed.

"Good thing our friends have amazing kids." Mom smiled. "Just like us."

Dad nodded.

I licked my lips. "For how long? I mean, how long is your vacation?"

Dad shrugged. "Don't worry, sweetie, you'll be the first to know."

Epilogue

Dayna grumbled when she gazed at the name of her roommate. "This really sucks, you know. I liked being your roommate."

Luna laughed. "Sorry, but it would be weird not being Pebble's roommate. You should've done what Conner did and signed up to be an RA this year. Then you wouldn't have a roommate."

"But then we wouldn't all be on the same floor."

I smiled at them. "It's July, we have time before we're moving into the dorms. Can we all just agree to be excited that we're taking a week off to visit California?"

Luna shook her head. "This is more for you than us, you get that, right? This is your family."

"It's also part of the training. We're supposed to visit each of the packs and see how the other alphas manage their wolves. Usually this is done prior to us becoming alphas, and we usually get more than a week per pack, but this is what time we can afford."

Over the intercom, our flight was announced. A sense of pure joy filled me as we got in line. It had only been about a year, but so much had happened. Luna leaned in close. "Do you think your sister will fly with me?"

A laugh bubbled out of me. "I'll tease her until she does. I'm guessing her alphas will help encourage her, too."

That was now my dream. I was so jealous that Jade could fly. I'd always been a bit jealous, but now that I was mated to a shifter, I couldn't believe I would be missing out on half of her experiences.

When we got to San Francisco International Airport, Owen waited for us. I flew at him, tackling him in a hug. He was one of the few people who'd always meant safety to me. It had always been him and Jade, then when I got older, Hollis had been added to the list.

Now that I was an adult, there were a lot of people on my list, but Owen and Jade, they'd been the first.

"Hiya, sis, I'm glad to see you too." He gazed at me. "You okay?"

The smile I gave him was as big as I could make it. "I am. I just ... I have things to tell you and the gang. Not here, though." I quickly introduced him to Luna and Dayna.

We drove to Were House, the name of their pack den. Fern, Conner, and Hollis had been living with the California pack for a month. The two epsilons were training with Jade, and Hollis because ... well, California.

When we entered, everyone was there, ready with big hugs, including a small army of toddlers.

Once we got through the first wave of welcomes, we changed into swimsuits and headed out to the hot tub. I asked Jade and Owen to join me because I had something serious to tell them. Bevin and José joined, which was fine, they could know any secret I had. Luna came to give me support. The others all headed for the pool.

Before I could start, Owen shook his head. "So, Mom and Dad really don't want to be alphas anymore?"

Luna laughed. "We brought the pack up for a training weekend. It was after Conner and Fern had found their panthers, so we could add that to the schedule. Anyway, while we were there, they explained to the pack that they would continue to help with the big things, your dad will continue with programs—gods above, he loves doing that— but beyond that they were retired in all ways, as alphas and from their jobs."

The others in the hot tub were amazed with the story.

After that, I told them about all the memories I had picked up over the last few months. I explained about my parents and becoming a wolf. I explained about my first shift and my first premonitions and my first impressions of them.

Through much of it, my eyes misted. Some of the memories I hadn't spoken aloud, though Luna knew them all. In the end, everyone was quiet, but the support was there.

Jade pulled me into her lap and gave me a fierce hug. Owen came in behind me, sandwiching me in a sibling hug. "I always wondered about your past, but never wanted to push. You were always scared of the memories."

Owen's support was just as important as Jade's. He rubbed my head. "Hey, wolf inside there. Thank you for letting her know we were there for her. We've always wanted nothing but the best for her, and you were right that we loved her from the start."

I could feel my second soul buzzing in my body. I smiled up at Owen, my wolf perking up within me. He winked back at me.

Bevin's somber voice cut through the tension. "Our wolves really are remarkable. I remember thinking when you returned to Wisconsin that all any of us wanted was for you to grow up. It was unheard of, you know, a kid with a developed wolf surviving to adulthood. It became the pack's mission."

"It's why I wanted to join all of you. You were always the people who protected me the most, made me feel the safest." I leaned back and felt Luna's arm around me. "But now that I'm an adult, I can protect myself. It's scary." I shot Luna a quick smile. "But like all of you, I've found my people."

There was a buzz as the emotions ran through the group. José smiled. "Pebble, you've done the pack and yourself proud. Spending time with some of your people, I like them too. The Wisconsin pack is going to do well with all of you leading the way."

I wanted to break up the intensity of emotion, so I smiled a bit wickedly at Jade. "So, sis, since *I* can't fly with Luna, I think you should."

Jade froze and glared at me. "You want me to fly with a goose? Really? You *know* there will be a video of this, and it'll be used against me."

Everyone laughed, but I pushed. "So what? Geese are used against you no matter what. And as I said, I can't fly with her, so you have to for me."

The sides of José's mouth twitched. "You know she's not wrong, chica. Think of it as a bonding opportunity."

Jade's face scrunched up. "Fine, but I think getting Pebble a swan would be a better solution."

I laughed. "I don't live here. That's not an option."

Bevin nodded. "She's not wrong. Whereas the Director is looking for volunteers, it's only for people in the area."

Shortly after that, we got out of the hot tub. We all sat in the pool chairs and watched as Jade and Luna took to the skies. A black swan and a goose. The air show had us all in stitches. And Fern made sure to record it all.

Thank you for reading Zephyr!
Please leave a review <u>online</u>.

Check out my <u>website</u> to find all the links to my socials
and find information on my next series!

Coming Soon:

- A new dystopian fantasy series: Aura Of The Chameleon

  Ivy is alone in the world, trying to survive without

  people questioning her magic. Petra lives with her dad,

  though after her mom was caught lying by the

  government, his reprogramming meant he'd never be

  the same. After meeting at work, can the two trust each

  other enough to share their biggest secrets? Are they

  strong enough to fight for better lives for themselves?

About the Author

Huckleberry Rahr is a mathematics instructor at the University of Wisconsin-Whitewater. She spent many years teaching math around the Midwest and in Papua New Guinea with the Peace Corps. Her parents instilled a love of reading from a young age.

She grew up with lesbian moms who had a huge collection of women authors with heroines as the protagonist. Her favorite genre was fantasy and science fiction, that is, until she discovered urban fantasy. What her mom's library lacked were books with characters that looked like her family: diversity in background, gender identity, and sexuality. She decided if she couldn't find that series, then she would write it.